"You are sitting and smoking;
you believe that you are sitting in your pipe,
and that *your pipe* is smoking *you*;
you are exhaling *yourself* in bluish clouds.
You feel just fine in this position,
and only one thing gives you worry or concern:
how will you ever be able to get out of your pipe?"

— Charles Baudelaire (Artificial Paradises)

The Phenomenalist

by

Conrad Aragon

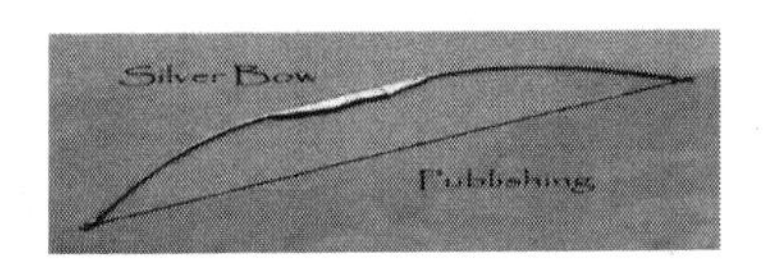

720 – Sixth Street, Box # 5
New Westminster, BC
V3C 3C5 CANADA

Title: The Phenomenalist
Author: Conrad Aragon
Publisher: Silver Bow Publishing
Cover Art: "Aladdin in the Land of the Lamp"
by Candice James
Edited: Sharla Cuthbertson

www.silverbowpublishing.com
info@silverbowpublishing.com

ISBN: 9781774030509 Print Book
ISBN: 9781774030516 E-Book

Library and Archives Canada Cataloguing in Publication

Title: The phenomenalist / by Conrad Aragon.
Names: Aragon, Conrad, 1945- author.
Identifiers: Canadiana (print) 20190120371 | Canadiana (ebook) 20190120398 | ISBN 9781774030509 (softcover) | ISBN 9781774030516 (HTML)
Classification: LCC PS3601.R34 P54 2019 | DDC 813/.6—dc23

Dedication

For Lorraine, without whose love, patience and friendship
this novel would never have been finished.

For my beloved children, Justin and Raquel.

For my beautiful grandchildren,
Oscar, Mariela and Valentina

Acknowledgments

My thanks to the two best writing coaches
an aspiring writer could hope for,
my brother Joseph Aragon
and my writing instructor Robert Eversz.

"Consciousness is that which is not the datum. Yet there is, of course, a sense in which consciousness is later *made* a datum. For we can be conscious of our consciousness."
W. T. Stace, *The Nature of the World, An Essay in Phenomenalist Metaphysics.*

"I believe that 'consciousness', when once it has evaporated to the estate of pure diaphaneity, is on the point of disappearing altogether. It is the name of a nonentity and has no right to a place among first principles. Those who still cling to it are clinging to a mere echo, the faint rumor left behind by the disappearing 'soul' upon the air of philosophy."
William James, *Essays in Radical Empiricism.*

"In the psychology of our unconscious there are typical figures that have a definite life of their own. All this is explained by the fact that the so-called unity of consciousness is an illusion. It is really a wish-dream. We like to think that we are one; but we are not, most decidedly not.
C. G. Jung, *Analytical Psychology, Its Theory & Practice.*

One

"Hello, Karl," I say, inches from his body.

Karl looks at me, puzzled. He's thinking, how does he know my name, and why has he spoken to me?

How do I know what he's thinking? Because I've always known what he's thinking, even before he knows what he's thinking, before he can give voice to his thoughts.

He stares at me. And now he's thinking, who is this strange person, and why is he gazing at me? Naturally, he doesn't recognize me, even though I've followed him for years, practically his shadow. What's more I'm not using any of my many clever disguises.

At this instant he decides I'm a busybody and walks away. One day, no doubt, he will see me, and his mind will connect with mine. It's an eventuality I dread, for reasons too complex to unravel here, and I hope to postpone it as long as possible. But for now, at least, I'm satisfied that day of reckoning is in the far distant future.

I met Karl long ago and was drawn to him. So much so that I began to observe his movements, gradually at first, then with dogged persistence until I knew everything about him. I couldn't, at first, explain my fascination with him. Then it hit me: I could read his mind. In the beginning, it was like tuning a radio, first getting static, then, after tweaking the knobs of my imaginary radio, I could clearly make out the voices in his head.

When I first began to observe Karl years ago, he was known as Milo, Milo Miller. Later, when he insisted on being called Karl, I continued to watch him, with practiced stealth, to eavesdrop on his private, most intimate conversations, and to observe his interactions with others.

It is indeed rare, this aptitude I possess, to read another's mind as if it were my own. It's both a privilege and a burden. I'm responsible for Karl. It falls to me to make sense of his existence, and, if necessary, to intercede when it is in peril.

Today is Saturday, and Karl awakens in his apartment in Alexandria, washes up, gets dressed, then strolls down to the river, reaching the small waterfront café where he settles into his favorite spot in the patio area, waiting for his customary cup of coffee, gazing aimlessly at the rushing waters of the Potomac.

Having followed Karl to the café, I take a seat at another table on the opposite end of the patio. I'm disguised as a bus driver, with thick, dark eyeglasses, a worn flat cap with visor, rumpled and faded grey uniform, and thick rubber-soled shoes. I'm drinking a morning coffee, hiding behind sheets of newsprint. The waiter has come to freshen my coffee, but I wave him off. Having followed Karl here so often, I know this waiter is called Jeremiah.

Jeremiah catches sight of Karl, seated at his customary table, and, knowing Karl's preferences, scurries into the kitchen, emerging with his coffee and a fresh copy of the Alexandria Times. He wordlessly places them on the small table before him.

"Thank you, Arthur," Karl manages to utter, momentarily emerging from his quiet meditations.

"Oh, no," the waiter answers, chuckling, "I'm called Jeremiah. Not Arthur."

"Quite right," Karl confesses, "I've mistaken you for someone else. I'm so sorry."

I'm not surprised that Karl has mistaken Jeremiah for Arthur, the head waiter at Chez Albert, who bears a striking resemblance to Jeremiah. I, too, have made the same mistake in my encounters with Jeremiah and Arthur.

"I understand, monsieur," Jeremiah replies, "no need to apologize, ha, ha. It's not the first time I've been called by that name, and, if you wish, you may call me by that name whenever it suits you. A name is of no consequence, after all. It's just a marker, here today and gone tomorrow. Ha, ha. And, in any event, the name Jeremiah…."

Jeremiah goes on and on about his name. But Karl doesn't hear a word of it. He is, by this time, lost in the extensive, secret chambers of his mind. From my listening post at the other end of the patio, some twenty to forty feet away, I tune in to his thoughts.

Random memories scurry through the tangled coils of his brain. A recent evening of pleasure with his soon to be bride, Tereza, a heated discussion about literature over dinner with his sometime roommate, Wallace Rust Wallace, the Third, an extremely large person with black, bushy mustache, the edges vaguely resembling tusks, which droop down well past his chin. Karl has dubbed him Wally the Walrus, an apt sobriquet for so imposing a human leviathan.

He falls further into a reverie, letting his mind wander unchecked, savoring a cascade of dreams, memories, and fictions. The cup of coffee and the Times are left untouched, abandoned, like artifacts of a different time and place; as though they are nothing more than the insignificant totems of an anonymous sojourner.

To look at him sitting there, relaxed, a smile on his lips, gazing out upon the river below, without a care, no one would guess that tomorrow is his wedding day.

Two

The next day Karl finds himself in the flowery courtyard of an old church outside of Alexandria where he is to be married. He arrives early and looks around, taking in the quaint venue that Tereza has chosen for the wedding ceremony. Guests have taken every available seat, so he doesn't notice me in the furthest row back from the altar, this time disguised as a medical assistant, in green surgical scrubs, white nurse's shoes, and mousy brown wig with matching mustache. To my relief, even at a distance of over a hundred feet I can still hear the voices in Karl's head.

He's looking forward to his union with Tereza. It's been days since their last meeting. Her absence was caused by a last-minute decision to journey to Prague to fetch her father for the wedding. Her father promised her he would make the journey, but as the date drew near, he announced he wouldn't come unless she accompanied him. Unable to convince him otherwise, Tereza made the long journey. It was supposed to be a quick trip, but problems with visas and passports caused delays.

It's now 11 a.m., when the ceremony was supposed to begin. The priest looks impatiently at his wristwatch, and mutters something which Karl cannot hear. From the expression on his face, it's clear to Karl that whatever he said was not flattering either to the bride or to the groom.

Wallace, the one Karl imagines as a walrus, stands to Karl's right. He flashes Karl a huge smile, and Karl reflexively smiles back, feeling a growing sense of unease. Although Wally is a friend of long standing and an occasional roommate, Karl can't help thinking that someone else has taken his place as best man. It doesn't matter that the man standing next to him looks and talks just like Wally the Walrus. He can't shake a growing suspicion that the man next to him is an imposter. It's a strange sensation, and one he's never before experienced, at least not as long as I've been reading his thoughts.

What's gotten into me? Karl wonders, as beads of sweat form on his brow. Should I demand that this imposter identify himself?

But his troubling thoughts are thankfully interrupted by a commotion at the rear of the courtyard. Karl turns and sees, with a sigh of relief, that Tereza has just entered the courtyard from the street entrance. A ragtag ensemble of musicians, kazoos, tambourines, fiddles, and accordions announce her arrival with an appropriate fanfare.

All of the guests have risen from their chairs and Karl is unable to see Tereza's face clearly. He's anxious to make sure it's his Tereza, although he doesn't understand where this nettlesome uncertainty over identity comes from. He dares not look over at his best man, still unsettled by the feeling that whoever that person is, standing where the best man should be, it's not the real Wally the Walrus.

Meanwhile, the bride glides down the center aisle toward him. On either side of the aisle are rows of folding chairs for the wedding guests. On one side, friends of the groom and the groom's best man, on the other, those of the bride who far outnumber the groom's guests. Although, in fairness, the groom's guests are much larger in height and girth, several of them mustachioed in the style of the best man, their massive buttocks taking up two chairs for every one chair occupied by the diminutive bride's guests. Except for Tereza's father, there is no family present among the guests. Karl has lost touch with all his family members, only occasionally receiving cryptic notes and messages from uncles, aunts, and cousins who are all variously named by letters of the alphabet instead of Christian names.

As Tereza approaches, he sees that she wears a simple peasant dress, leaning lightly on the arm of a smallish gentleman whom Karl correctly infers is Tereza's father, although he has yet to meet him. Under a crown of multi-colored flowers, the bride's eyes glow. Her upper lip is shaped like Cupid's bow, and she smiles openly at Karl. As her gaze settles on him, her eyelids flutter as if she were about to receive a lover's kiss. He has to admit she is quite lovely, but he can't help thinking there is something different about her, something foreign that he can't quite decipher.

Is this really Tereza, or someone who just looks like her, he wonders.

"Everything okay?" asks the man at his side whom Karl believes is impersonating Wally the Walrus.

That's it, it's the imposter's voice, Karl thinks. It's not Wally's voice. He looks at the best man. He looks at the bride. In his mind, something is terribly wrong.

The strangeness of it all threatens to overwhelm him, and he looks up at the church bell tower which looms overhead, closing his eyes, wishing he were up there so as to contemplate the scene with indifference.

And then, suddenly, he feels his mind slip away from his body, and, in his mind's eye, he is up there, leaning out over a narrow ledge of the bell tower.

I, too, feel my body separate from my mind. We are like marooned specters, without any substance, without any weight, unbearably light, looking down on Karl's soulless body. The body he's just abandoned in the courtyard below him twitches and natters like an automaton whose wiring has been crossed, throwing out barely discernible sparks. My own body, devoid of consciousness, is slumped in its chair in the last row of guest chairs where I left it.

"Which of us is real," I hear Karl mutter, "I who have no body, or that grotesque homunculus down there? And who are those imposters who resemble Tereza and Wally?"

We, that is, Karl and I, gaze at his simulacrum planted in the middle of a peculiar scene unfolding below the bell tower. The altar, through his freshly altered perception, is nothing more than a crude proscenium upon which play actors, including Tereza, Wally, and his vacuous simulacrum, are lined up in their assigned places, waiting to enact their prescribed roles.

Where is the professor of this Punch and Judy show? I can't help wondering. I glance at Karl to make sure he hasn't read my thoughts, or, for that matter, detected my ghostly presence.

He remains oblivious to me and to the contents of my mind.

Meanwhile, below us, the extremely large person with the bushy mustache who is impersonating Wally the Walrus tugs at the automaton's sleeve, as if to alert him to some impending event. But the empty shell which once housed Karl's mind does not move, although its twitching and nattering has by now ceased.

Karl imagines some appropriate bridal music in the air, but he hears nothing except for the distant, muffled beating of the automaton's heart.

At that moment the bride reaches the automaton's side and slips her slender hand smoothly into the crook of his arm. He, or more appropriately, it, remains standing stiffly, eyes fixed to the front, a blank expression on its face.

The priest's lips move, then the bride's lips move as if in response, their heads and bodies moving like marionettes, following some long disused call and response.

His hearing returns just as the bride says, "Yes, Father, I do."

Her father, standing to her left, smiles broadly, beaming with pride, his bushy eyebrows raised above wide eyes, the eyeball of one made of glass, his lips parted, exposing several polished silver teeth which gleam in the sunlight, his nose hairs bristling as he breathes.

The priest turns to the automaton.

"And do you, Karl, take Tereza to be your wedded wife?"

There is no response from the empty shell with a vacant brainpan. The priest repeats his question, this time in a loud, threatening voice, leaning in toward Karl. Still the automaton does not or cannot answer.

The father of the bride shakes the arm of the automaton violently, shouting and gesticulating. The best man has a look of consternation written upon his large face. The priest, ever more agitated, continues to shout at the inanimate thing, as the wedding guests in their folding chairs become restless. Then a menacing murmur runs among them, several of them frantically making the sign of the cross.

The father of the bride cuffs the automaton on the ear, pushing the bride aside in the act with such violence that she cries out, staggering backward and nearly losing her balance.

The best man, seeing his inert companion battered in this fashion, retaliates, reaching across Karl's body to land a heavy blow to the side of the bride's father's head, and, in the process, he knocks the automaton to the ground with his massive shoulders as he leans in to deliver the blow.

The bride, regaining her balance, flees the scene in a panic, sobbing as she hurriedly makes her way to the church entrance. Meanwhile the bride's father strikes back at the best man, both combatants now earnestly engaged in a free-for-all.

The wedding guests are on their feet, shouting insults at one another. Some have moved into the aisles, pushing and shoving, cursing. Someone throws a chair and it strikes an old woman, and she tumbles to the ground, blood spurting from her head and arching gracefully over the heads of nearby guests.

The priest joins the fray, wielding a large wooden crucifix which he expertly deploys against not only the combatants, but also upon Karl, who is lying dazed and bloodied on the ground.

Three

When he regains consciousness, Karl is no longer in the courtyard of a small church. He's a patient in a hospital bed. I, too, am hovering nearby, this time in the guise of an orderly, collecting bed pans, mopping up blood, vomit, and other unsavory excreta.

I must say, I hope you will not rely on me to reveal my occult presence and the disguises I adopt in every one of the scenes I choose to narrate from Karl's life. May I rely on you simply to assume that, whatever the situation, I am there in one form or another?

As for Karl, lying semiconscious on his hospital bed, he remembers nothing about the wedding debacle except what I have just set down in writing. He, too, wrote about it much later, as his memory pieced together fragments of the event, in tablets, notebooks, and upon scraps of newsprint, napkins, torn envelopes, post-its, whatever was at hand.

Dazed and confused from heavy doses of pain medication, and in constant discomfort, Karl looks up and sees Wally the Walrus standing nearby.

"Feeling better?" Wally asks, smiling.

"How long have I been here? Where is Tereza?"

"Take it easy, old chum. You've been through quite a shock and have been in a coma for a week. The doctors called me when you began to show improved brain function. I was so relieved, I rushed right over."

"A week?" Karl gasps. "I've been out.... Where's Tereza? Is she all right? Why isn't she here?"

"She's fine. Don't worry about her. I'm sure she'll come as soon as she can. She had to return...."

But Karl doesn't hear the rest of Wally's sentence. Overcome by massive doses of narcotics, he falls, once again, into a deep sleep.

Hours later, he wakes again with a start and sees a small man bending over him, as if examining a corpse.

Am I dead? Karl is thinking, slowly coming-to. The small man bending over him comes into sharper focus.

"Ah, you're a psychotherapist!" Karl exclaims, now fully alert, temporarily forgetting his aches and pains, and demonstrating an uncanny ability to discern the man's profession.

But the therapist either chooses to ignore Karl's outburst, or does not hear him. He strikes Karl as an odd looking fellow, bald, short and pudgy, with a pointed goatee. He is sporting wire rim glasses and coughing incessantly. He looks, remarkably, like Lenin. Not that Karl ever met Lenin. But he once admired a portrait of the man hanging in some obscure eastern European museum showing Lenin in profile with that pointy beard.

He's excited to see the psychotherapist, even if he desists from uttering aloud his inner thoughts concerning the therapist's appearance.

I've busied myself in an adjoining bathroom, where I can follow the colloquy between Karl and his therapist. Although the therapist caught sight of me when he entered Karl's room, he takes no further notice of me.

"How are we today?" asks the therapist.

The question confuses Karl. Why has the therapist referred to him as we and not as you? Am I more than one person? he wonders, or has the therapist intended to include himself in the question?

Just then he catches sight of his own face, replicated in a mirror affixed to a door near his bed. The image is his, but not the expression it wears. The face in the mirror is grimacing, displaying an unsightly, twisted expression of disgust. He looks away from the image and touches his own face, tracing the upturned corners of his lips, and realizes that, unlike his image, he's smiling. When he glances back at the mirror, the image is gone.

This reflection of himself at that moment is particularly unfortunate, and, together with the therapist's confusing question, prompts him to reconsider nagging questions about the phenomenology of self, about identity, the continuity of consciousness, and, more particularly, the existence of body doubles.

Karl refuses to admit that body doubles exist, even though I have observed an encounter between him and a body double from which he fled in haste, burying the memory in the deepest, darkest recesses of his mind.

Unlike Karl, I am satisfied that body doubles exist. After all, how rare and extraordinary can it be that one human should resemble another? Genetically speaking and given the history of our species and the inevitable replication of identical genetic sequences, it would be extraordinary if there were not a plethora of identical humans coexisting across the globe.

But it isn't just the possibility that doubles exist that Karl finds perplexing. He's also troubled by the absence of a proper lexicon for the occasion.

In engaging a double in conversation, assuming such things exist, he muses, should I refer to him as You, or as It, or as He, or as I? Or, he reasons, since there are two of me, should I use the plural We, instead of the singular I?

Karl's thoughts are interrupted by the piercing gaze of that strange looking therapist. Have I been thinking aloud, he wonders, or has the doctor guessed my thoughts?

Whatever the case, the doctor straightens up, having grown weary of bending over him and closely examining his physiognomy through the lens of a magnifying glass attached to a headband awkwardly affixed to his forehead.

"Can you be in two places at the same time?" the therapist asks.

"No." Karl lies, knowing that to admit the possibility of being in two places at once entails an admission that body doubles are a reality.

"Is he lying?" the clever doctor asks, introducing the third personal pronoun, still hoping to draw Karl into a futile exercise in sophistry by multiplying the number of persons in the room.

"I have no idea what you mean, doctor," he replies, hoping to dissuade him from further probing.

"Umm, hmm," murmurs the doctor. He carefully removes the ridiculously oversized magnifying glass from his brow and packs it into his bag. Then he moves briskly to the door without another word.

But he stops abruptly when Karl blurts out, "Doctor! Doctor! What is your diagnosis?"

"Always with the diagnosis!" the therapist puffs, his face reddening. "Very well, if you must know, you have suffered a psychotic break."

"What can I do to get better?" Karl asks.

"Suicide, comrade, is always an option. But no, in this case my advice, at least for the present, is, take two aspirin and call me in the morning, and stay away from mirrors," he adds.

"But I don't have your number," Karl protests, rising slightly and scanning a nearby night stand for pen and paper. "What is your number?" he asks, more insistently.

"Nine," the doctor retorts. "The number is nine."

He drops a business card on a side table next to Karl's bed, then he walks out of the room, softly humming a Viennese waltz. Karl picks it up and reads aloud, "Dr. Sax, Number 9, Alexandria."

He knows instantly that the number nine is code for some meaning he cannot yet discern, and not a street address.

While Karl is distracted, I quietly slip out of the bathroom and follow the therapist, my curiosity aroused by his unusual therapeutic approach.

On his way to the elevators, he stops at the nurses' station to retrieve a bowler hat which he takes in his hands.

"Come along Olivia," he says, gently brushing his hat brim.

A coterie of nurses, who are familiar with the little therapist and his strange behaviors, assemble to watch him as he departs. As soon as the elevator doors close on him, they burst out laughing, elbowing each other. As they break away from one another to resume their appointed duties, one nurse vigorously brushes the shoulders of a companion.

"Come along, Olivia," he says to renewed gales of laughter.

However absurd the good doctor appeared to the hospital staff, he struck Karl as quite astute and competent, and, examining his business card, he made up his mind to consult Dr. Sax as soon as he was able.

Four

Karl's discharged from the hospital at last, and I observe him as he returns to his apartment in Alexandria. Although he must use crutches to get around, he is otherwise well on his way to complete recovery from his injuries. Once inside, he inspects every room, and finds nothing amiss, only slightly disappointed there is no message from Tereza, and that Wally the Walrus, his sometime roommate, isn't home.

Days pass, and still neither Tereza nor Wally have been to visit him. Although Karl is in love with Tereza, and is fond of Wally, he finds it best not to think of them. The eerie feeling he experienced in the church courtyard that each was somehow different, foreign, together with what he explains away as an out of body experience, contribute to his reluctance to reach out to either.

With or without Tereza or Wally, Karl feels completely at peace with the world, alone with his musings, spinning stories in his head like a literate spider spinning literate webs. He was, and is, you see, a writer of fiction, and making up stories gives him an escape from his ever-unsettled mind.

But lately, to add to his mental distress, and in spite of his best efforts to stay busy with pleasant tasks instead of obsessing over the troubling memories roiling his mind, he's become curiously nervous around doors. What fiction is this, he wonders, that affects my sleep and my nerves? What lurks behind the closed doors?

He sees me standing outside his front door, this time disguised as a mailman, a fake mailbag draped over my shoulder. It doesn't occur to him to ask what I'm doing lurking on his doorstep.

"You there," he calls out to me from an open window.

"Yes, you there. Please open the front door. No, it's not locked. That's it. Come in, please."

I follow his instructions and enter through the front door. He glances at me without any hint that he knows me.

"Will you please remove all the doors?" He points to the inside doors, many of which are closed. "I'll make it worth your while."

"Yes, sir, my pleasure," I reply putting down my fake mailbag. It doesn't take a mind reader to know that he's taken me for a handyman, my mailbag for a toolkit. He brings me some trail mix and a bottle of water and leaves me to the task.

"What about the front door?" I ask, after I've removed all the interior doors.

"No, no. Leave that one in place, but don't close it on your way out. Here," he says, handing me a wad of currency.

I'm about to protest but decide not to, taking the proffered sum without comment and leaving.

Alone in his apartment with no interior doors, Karl begins to look with growing dread at the one remaining door, the front door which I absent-mindedly closed when I left him. With that door closed, he's unable to leave his apartment in search of Tereza, with whom he's had no contact since his discharge from the hospital.

"It's all too absurd," he scolds himself, "this ridiculous fear of mine about doors."

He is of two minds on the subject, as was Dostoyevsky's Raskolnikov over the murder of Alyona Ivanova, justifying his criminal acts while at the same time burdened by guilt and self-doubt.

On the one hand, Karl freely admits the absurdity of his fear of doors and wishes to free himself of it; on the other, he clings to it, embracing the odd comfort it confers in temporarily assuaging a persistent and unreasoned angst of unknown origin.

Briefly ruminating on this absurdity, he courageously vows to take action to reform himself. Thus, it comes to pass one day that Karl approaches the closed front door. He grabs hold of the doorknob before the panic can set in and opens it with one mighty heave.

Sometime later a passerby, whose name, I know for a fact to be Franz, incidentally, prods him back into consciousness, lifting his limp body from the pavement and dragging him up a few steps to his doorstep.

The appearance of that passerby is no accident. He is one of Karl's body doubles who is returning home when he encounters his alternate-self sprawled, face down, on the ground like an inebriated derelict.

Out of compassion for the unconscious body lying there, and not yet aware of the resemblance between himself and the person lying at his feet, half on the sidewalk and half in the street, Franz drags Karl to the front entrance of his apartment. This is no small feat considering the three high cement steps he first has to surmount to get there.

He's about to drag him inside through the doorless apartment entrance when he realizes that the body he's struggling with is the body of his body double. He's shocked, drops the body instantly, and runs away in a panic. He does not return to his apartment for three weeks, by which time, much to his relief, his body double has vanished.

Although I observed the event, I cannot competently aver which was Franz, and which was Karl. I suppose the dilemma is best resolved by allowing that each was the double of the other, and both were Karl.

What I can attest to with certainty is, watching the scene unfold, I was amazed, as if watching some heinous crime committed before my very eyes. Although I know that body doubles exist, to see them interacting, occupying nearly the same space at the same moment in time is disconcerting, to say the least.

In any event, what was clear from the incident, apart from the shock it caused me, is that Karl's plan for overcoming his aversion to doors was to no avail.

Five

Out for a stroll along the crowded cobblestone streets of Alexandria, on a pleasant afternoon, Karl catches sight of Tereza peering into the window of a small shop just a few blocks away.

Casting aside all his doubts and fears inspired by the events at the church courtyard, he hurries toward her just as she turns away from the shop window.

"Tereza!" he calls out.

But she appears not to have heard him and doesn't turn around. Instead, she continues briskly on her way.

He follows, his heart pounding in wild anticipation, since their separation has been intolerably long. The streets are crowded, and he nearly loses sight of her when she stops to greet a very large person whom she embraces, and, arm and arm with the anonymous stranger, she steps into a waiting cab.

Karl is both sad and mystified. Was it truly Tereza? he wonders, or someone who looks just like her? And if it was Tereza, why didn't she acknowledge me? And who was the large person she met?

He releases his mind of these troubling thoughts and resumes his stroll along the cobblestone streets of old Alexandria. He continues in the direction of the river, thinking now of his favorite riverfront café and the fine Lager he'll request which will be served by his favorite waiter, Jeremiah.

As he approaches the café, he sees the very large man resembling the man he's just seen embracing a woman resembling Tereza before entering a cab with her. He is sitting at a table—Karl's favorite table as it turns out—reading the Alexandria Times. He moves irresistibly to that table when the large man, setting his newspaper aside, suddenly rises to greet him.

"Karl!" he exclaims. "What a pleasure! It's me, Wallace! Come join me!"

Karl is not overjoyed at the sight of Wally the Walrus.

Although he brushed aside his recent pursuit of a woman he thought was Tereza as nothing more than a case of mistaken identity, it resurrected his earlier fears that the bride who appeared at the church courtyard ceremony was not his Tereza, nor was the best man his longtime friend, Wally the Walrus.

He approaches leerily, searching the countenance of the man sitting at his table, looking for some sign that might betray him as an imposter.

Despite his doubts about the true identity of Wally the Walrus, he nevertheless sits at the table, and, after several mugs of Lager, he is convinced that his table companion is the real Wally the Walrus. They are soon lost in a discussion regarding certain obscure passages from the Book of Genesis; especially the story of Onan, one of Judah's three sons, his two other sons being called Er and Shelah.

According to the biblical text, Judah's first son, called Er, who had taken a wife, called Tamar, had been thoughtlessly struck dead for some unspecified evil deeds before impregnating his new bride. Tamar was greatly displeased at this turn of events, having counted on a male heir to secure her position in Judah's household.

Judah, and Judah's God, who was called God—but whose name was Yahweh—, then commanded Judah's second son, called Onan, to wed Er's widow, to lie with her, to plant his seed in her, and to raise up children in his dead brother's name.

But Onan defied both his father and Yahweh by refusing to deposit his seed in his older brother's newly widowed wife, choosing instead to spill his seed on the ground, presumably after pleasuring Er's widow in every conceivable way, using every artifact at hand, including the one between his legs.

Yahweh and Judah were passing wroth when they discovered Onan's duplicity, and, for his defiance, Onan was struck dead.

What did it all mean?

"Why, isn't it obvious?" Wally says. "This Onan fellow didn't want any little Onans running around. It's what you call a cautionary tale. If you don't want to replicate yourself as you're expected to do, and can't control the urge to masturbate, God himself will strike you as dead as a proverbial door nail."

"On the contrary," Karl replies. "Onan wants nothing more than to replicate by coupling with himself. His act of masturbation represents a perfect alignment of body and mind, without the intrusion of the alien consciousness required by the act of copulation. He engages in acts of self-gratification to allow his conscious mind to create a flawless imagined world, populated by his doppelganger, culminating in the ecstasy of orgasm and, incidentally, in the spilling of his body's by-product on the ground."

Karl's arguments prove far too subtle for Wally, who, barely taking notice, begins to drink copious amounts of beer, and summons Jeremiah, the waiter to request an extravagant dinner.

Undaunted by Wally's indifference, Karl continues his exegesis of Onan's story, shifting his focus onto Tamar's deceptions.

"Do you remember what happens after both of Judah's sons are struck down?"

Wally grunts an unintelligible response between morsels.

"Tamar, who's been cheated out a rightful heir by both of Judah's sons, decides to lie with her father-in-law Judah and begets a man child…."

By this time, Karl might as well be preaching to an empty temple. His audience of one is devouring platters full of food and doesn't hear a word of Karl's recitation. The only sounds Wally makes are the scraping of eating utensils on the surface of porcelain plates, and the moans and groans of a large animal chewing, gulping, sighing, burping, and farting.

Six

Karl stands before a mirror, studying his appearance. It's winter, so what he sees is a stocky, though not portly, middle aged man of average height and of swarthy complexion with onyx eyes, and a massive head of raven black hair vaguely suggestive of Mediterranean origins.

His appearance in winter is quite different from his appearance at any other season of the year. Commencing in the late Fall, he begins to grow a beard, achieving full bloom by mid-winter. He wears a dark overcoat, a black felt hat, and favors long stem tobacco pipes which he stores in the pockets of his coat, along with an ample supply of scented pipe tobacco.

By late spring he appears in public shorn of his beard, in light clothing, and smokeless. In summer, he trims his eyebrows and his abundant black hair, dons short sleeved shirts, chinos, boat shoes, dark glasses, and sports a diamond stud in his left ear lobe.

Seven

Still afflicted with his door phobia, Karl decides to visit Dr. Sax, the one who looks like Lenin.

Karl has several things on his mind, enigmas, more accurately, which he struggles in vain to comprehend. I'm tempted to intervene, to help free his mind of trouble, but decide against it. After all, I'm a stranger to Karl. I'd be compromised, never again able to observe and report on his movements anonymously. Moreover, I'm not convinced that such an encounter would be entirely free of violence. No doubt the time will come when I have no choice but to show myself, but all the circumstances persuade me that now is not an auspicious moment to do so.

I note, with growing concern, that the volume of his scribblings has increased during this time; a fairly reliable gauge of Karl's inner turmoil. It's all I can do to keep up. He worries over Tereza's disappearance, the out of body experience that ruined his wedding ceremony, his irrational fear that Tereza's and Wally's identities have mutated, and a vague foreboding that his consciousness has become fragmented, even shared with other bodies at different times and in different places.

In Karl's mind, compared to these enigmas, his door phobia is a pleasant distraction. So, rather than confronting his deeper concerns, he sets out for a consult with Dr. Sax about doors. He doesn't bother to make an appointment; instead, he walks toward central Alexandria, confident that instinct will guide him to the correct location, since, as is typical of him, he hasn't bothered to learn the good doctor's address.

After wandering around the busy downtown area, he chances upon an old nine story building in the Art Deco style prominently displaying an immense number 9 emblazoned on a large bronze plaque over the double glass doors.

"Ah, hah!" he exclaims, "I've found it!"

He opens those doors without any difficulty—they're made of glass, you see—and passes through them into the foyer, chances upon a building directory on the wall outside the elevator and discovers that Dr. Sax is on the ninth floor, suite number 9.

He refuses, of course, to take the elevator because of his fear of doors, and climbs the stairs, there being no closed door barring access to, and exit from the stairwell.

I busy myself in a small snack bar in the lobby until I see Karl enter and make for the stairs. I follow him at a good distance until he reaches the door to Dr. Sax's suite. He stands there quietly, waiting for someone to exit, leaving the door open long enough for him to scurry inside. Once he gains entry, I quietly enter the suite and find a chair in the crowded waiting room from which to observe him, well outside of his line of sight.

A strange odor permeates the waiting room, the walls of which are painted a bright orange. Random pictures hang askew on every wall depicting scenes from great works of literature. One shows poor Raskolnikov in the slain pawnbroker's room with a bloody hatchet in his hand, a twisted smile on his grizzled face. Another depicts Aeneas fornicating Dido in a dark cave while a storm rages just outside, dashing his Trojan fleet against the rocks along the Libyan coast.

The whole scene reminds me of the inside of a lunatic asylum I once had the privilege to visit for forty-eight hours. As a state inspector, mind you.

Karl sits in an oversized, overstuffed chair in the waiting room, and begins constructing a story based upon memories so vague that he cannot say they ever truly happened; events surrounding a trauma, a fall, and several blows to the head and body, administered by an irate curate wielding a crucifix as if vanquishing infidel Saracens.

He's almost worked his way through what he's confident are verifiable events of his recent past when the inner door to the doctor's private office opens and a casually dressed man emerges; a patient, no doubt, whose consultation has just ended. Although the man resembles Jeremiah, Karl is quite sure that it is not Jeremiah but rather his look-alike, Arthur, mainly because the logo, Chez Albert, is emblazoned on the shirt he's wearing.

Karl is so startled at seeing Arthur, in so unlikely a place, that he immediately drops the stylus and abandons the tablet upon which he's been furiously writing.

"Hey! You there," he blurts out. "You there, the waiter from Chez Albert!"

When the waiter from Chez Albert doesn't respond, he calls out, "Arthur! It's me, Karl! Don't you know me, Arthur?"

A look of madness lights Arthur's face, and he collapses, sobbing, onto a nearby couch.

"Do you suppose that any self-respecting poet would wish to be called out in public in such a fashion?" he cries out.

Dr. Sax runs out of his office into the waiting room to investigate, nearly tripping over the furniture in his haste. His face is a mask of clinical concern as he rushes to Arthur's side, sits next to the famous waiter from Chez Albert, and pulls him tenderly into his arms.

"There, there, Monsieur Arthur, we all know you are a famous poet, do we not?"

The doctor looks around for agreement, and everyone in the waiting room mumbles a polite assent, their eyes averted in embarrassment.

Then the doctor begins to recite from Arthur's famous poem, eyes closed as he rocks Arthur in his arms.

"Pauvre innocent! L'enfer ne peut attaquer les païens." Dr. Sax inhales deeply, eyes closed, as he continues to embrace the forlorn waiter-poet.

"C'est la vie encore! Plus tard, les delices de la damnation seront plus profondes, un crime, vite, que me tombe au néant, de par la loi humaine." [*Poor innocent! Pagans don't fear Hell. So long as one lives, one must put off the pleasures of Hell. So let me be quickly condemned to death for committing crimes under the laws of man.*]

Several of the waiting room patients are sniffling and wiping tears from their eyes. Karl begins to feel disconnected but remains steadfastly in his body.

Arthur sits upright and smiles, now completely in possession of himself. He approaches Karl and apologizes for his outburst.

Karl doesn't know how to respond, then notices that Dr. Sax is directing him, with hand signals, to follow him into his office. Karl points to the several other patients in the waiting room.

"Me?" he asks, surprised that Dr. Sax has taken him out of order, and without an appointment. "What about...?"

"Are you coming or not?"

With a shrug of his shoulders, Karl follows Dr. Sax. He's left his tablet and stylus on the floor next to the chair he was sitting in. Stealthily, taking pains not to be noticed, I pick them up from the floor and stuff them inside my overcoat. I look around and note that Karl has followed Dr. Sax into his private consulting room. There is no receptionist, and the check-in counter is vacant. I slither inside the small reception area and find a full-color monitor connected to a closed circuit camera inside Dr. Sax's chambers. I sit on the floor, blocked from view by a wall separating the small reception room from the still crowded waiting room and fix my gaze on the images flickering on the small screen.

Upon entering, Karl sinks into a large, ox-blood colored leather sofa, and gazes at the good doctor who is leaning against a great oaken desk, a look of impatience on his face. Karl is again struck by the therapist's peculiar appearance, rendered comical by the pince-nez on the bridge of his nose, the tuft of hair that runs like a narrow belt at the back of his shiny pate from ear to ear; a clown-sized bow tie at his neck rounding out his garish ensemble.

He can't help rudely staring at the therapist's pince-nez, nor can he hide the broad smirk on his face, barely restraining an urge to burst out laughing.

"I assume from your expression that you are amused?" Dr. Sax asks, frowning.

"I-I-I'm sorry, it's just that a pince-nez seems so, you'll think me rude but, out of place?"

"What pince-nez?"

He sweeps a hand up to his brow, dislodging the artifact from his nose. It clatters as it hits the tiled floor.

"I have no pince-nez."

"Yes," Karl dutifully responds, "you haven't a pince-nez."

"Very well then, comrade, down to business. I have a series of intake questions for you of great diagnostic value. Are you ready?"

Karl nods, a little nervous about what might follow, wishing he were someone else, far away. But he does not wish to find himself in two places at once. It's just too unpleasant, this detachment of mind from body. He thinks, I shall resist the urge to sever my consciousness from the space and time I now occupy. Besides, I'm curious about what the little therapist might do or say to me. I wish to remain fully aware and vigilant of my surroundings. Will he poke me with needles, ask me to disrobe, grasp my testicles, insert his fingers up my rectum? As he's lost in thought about these things, the doctor's voice invades his reverie.

"Do you react to a full moon?" Dr. Sax begins. He wears the mask of a clinician, and enunciates very precisely, holding a ledger in one hand, a pen in the other, taking notes from time to time.

"How do you mean?"

"It's a simple enough question," Dr. Sax continues, a note of irritation in his voice, "do you sit by the window and bay at the moon when it is full?"

"No," he replies, trying not to sneer as he speaks.

Dr. Sax looks at him suspiciously, apparently unconvinced by his answer.

"Do you run after fire trucks?"

"No, never."

"Have you ever had the urge to bite a postman?"

"Doctor, these are absurd questions! Do I look like a dog?"

Dr. Sax gives him a stern look.

"How many licensed psychotherapists do you see in this room?"

He obediently scans the room, noting that apart from Dr. Sax and himself, there isn't another living soul, assuming the existence of so quaint a thing as the soul.

"Yes, my smart fellow, it is just you and I. I am the therapist; you are the patient." Then he resumes where, presumably, he left off.

"Have you ever defecated while on all fours?"

Laughing, he replies that he has never done so. But then a distant memory intervenes.

"I take it back, I did so once as an Army recruit during a live fire exercise."

"Ah-ha! So, you admit that you were in the Army?"

"I didn't know my military service was an issue," he responds, thoroughly baffled.

Dr. Sax looks completely disgusted, tossing his notepad on the floor.

"I can see we're going nowhere with this!" He gets up from his chair and paces back and forth. Then he stops and regards Karl.

"You think this is some silly parlor game, I'll warrant." He glares at Karl. "Well, answer me!"

"I have to admit that all of this seems crushingly absurd," he answers, smiling from embarrassment rather than from amusement.

"You think so, but that silly parlor game has already given me a diagnosis. I know you suffer from januaphobia gravis, a fear of doors."

He's speechless, amazed that Dr. Sax has so quickly and precisely uncovered his fear of doors.

"It's plain enough. But you mustn't think it so rare or exceptional. In the Soviet Union, during the time of Stalin, two in seven members of a farming collective had the same fear of closed doors; and in Moscow, where you would expect more interior doors, the ratio was closer to one in three. Yes, doors are universal signifiers; they have meaning. Jean Paul had the correct metaphor with his huis clos. Can you imagine him writing an entire play about a room whose doors were left open?"

How, Karl is thinking, can a door be a universal signifier; and what has Sartre got to do with it? The whole thing's absurd, he says to himself.

"Not absurd in the least," Dr. Sax responds vigorously.

He obviously reads minds, Karl thinks.

"If you think so, you must read Sartre more closely. But enough of this prattle. I have here a simple diagnostic tool that will prove the point, even to someone who has read too much Schopenhauer."

At this, Dr. Sax pulls a bunch of photographs from a desk drawer. He squints to see them but can't do so until he opens another drawer and pulls out a monocle which he holds up to his right eye.

Karl dares not mention the monocle.

Dr. Sax shuffles the photos like a deck of cards, then pulls one out and hands it to him.

"Tell me what you see."

"A glass door, the entrance to a nine-story art deco building. This very building, I believe."

"Does the door in that photograph cause you any fear, comrade?"

"No fear whatever, this door would be quite easy to open. I can see what's on the other side of it." Yet another absurd test, he tells himself.

Dr. Sax looks up as though he's read Karl's thoughts but declines to respond. Instead, he hands him another photo showing a door on display for sale in a hardware store.

What lies beyond that door is too obvious to imagine. It's a play door, one that Karl feels is completely devoid of menace or mystery.

"No problem," he says, feeling a bit bored by so futile an exercise.

"Look at this one," Dr. Sax continues, handing him a picture of a door lying flat in the dirt on some construction site. What lies under the door is too obvious to describe.

"It's of no consequence to me," he says with a shrug.

"And this one?" Dr. Sax passes him a picture of a closed door of solid oak affixed to a commercial building on a busy city street.

Karl swallows hard, doing his best to remain composed, convinced that on the other side of every such door lurks the threat of complete physical and mental annihilation.

"Yes, definitely. This is a door through which I may not pass...."

"Unless it is already open?" Dr. Sax finishes his thought.

"Exactly. I will not open such a door."

Dr. Sax scoops up the photos and throws them into a nearby waste basket.

"So now we know. Your phobia has only to do with solid, closed doors, which, as everyone knows, is nothing more than the fear of opening such a door and being swept away into that starry night of preconscious oblivion, as my teacher used to say."

Looking over his shoulder, Karl notices the portrait of Carl Jung on the wall behind him. The walls are otherwise bare, but there is a small framed photo of a smiling Lenin in profile on the doctor's desk.

Dr. Sax, whose eyes are closed, seems entirely to have forgotten that Karl is still present.

"You're free to leave; we're quite finished with the diagnosis," Dr. Sax says, as if not only suddenly aware of, but annoyed by his continued existence.

"But doctor, what can be done to cure me of this phobia?"

"Nothing. Now please leave, you're becoming tiresome."

Karl feels alone and helpless, but then again, he always feels alone and helpless. It's all he can do to keep from crying.

"Very well then," the therapist says, noting Karl's obvious distress. "Lie down on the couch. Would you like some cannabis, mescaline, opium, lysergic acid?"

"No, thank you," he replies, reclining on the leather couch. From the corner of his eye, he sees Dr. Sax take some white pulpy substance from a side table and pop it into his mouth. He masticates vigorously for a moment, then turns toward Karl.

"Let's proceed with an exercise I know will be of value to you, comrade. Close your eyes and lay your hands across your chest as though you were a corpse ready for the embalmer."

He's reluctant to see himself as a corpse but, as the good doctor pointed out, he's the doctor; Karl is the patient.

"Now repeat after me. Shoo, shee, shoo, shee...."

Karl notices a large card propped up on the glass table next to the couch where his corpse is laid out. The card displays the Chinese characters for the mantra. It reads: 休息, 休息, 休息 [休息, "Take it easy, relax"], the characters used for the expression,

Shoo, shee, shoo, shee….

Karl has never studied Chinese, nor visited China, yet he knows what the characters are, as if he were Chinese, living in Chinese time and space, his conscious mind temporarily scrambled and rearranged. He can feel the synapses in his brain popping, his eyes opening and closing in uncontrollable spasms. Yet it does not seem at all extraordinary to him, just his body reacting to a non-malignant stimulus of unknown origin.

Karl dutifully follows suit, repeating the mantra dictated by Dr. Sax, "休息, 休息, 休息," for what seems well over an hour.

He grows weary of the exercise and, glancing in the little therapist's direction, sees through half closed eyes, that Dr. Sax is floating, his entire body rising above his chair until his bald head begins to bounce softly against the ceiling, like a child's accidentally released balloon.

Then Karl quietly rises and makes his way out to the street below. It's only when he reaches the sidewalk that he realizes, to his amazement, that he's opened all of the doors in the building on his way out, beginning with the door to Dr. Sax's inner sanctum.

"I'm cured!!!" he shouts gleefully, as he races for a waiting streetcar.

But the relief is temporary, I'm sad to report. By the time he reaches his apartment, he finds he cannot open the front door. He begins pounding on the door until, at last, Wally, who happens to be home, hears Karl and lets him in.

Eight

Karl sets aside the Times he's been reading in the living room of his apartment in Alexandria. He rises, turns down the lights in the room, and starts a fire in the hearth. Dark paneling covers two walls lined with books from floor to ceiling, a third wall facing the street has a bank of windows with louvered blinds, which he has shuttered. Centered in the wall opposite the windows is a good-sized brick fireplace opposite which are two matching leather armchairs.

Although he shares the apartment with Wally the Walrus, Wally happens to be away, his comings and goings being unpredictable. Karl plunks down on one of the two armchairs, enjoying the silence of his cozy living room and the glow of the bright fire warming the pores of his skin.

The silence is shattered by Wally's sudden appearance. He's just returned from another city where he's managing the production of one of his plays. He holds a bunch of letters and magazines he's retrieved from the letter box.

"Howdy!" Wally calls out, in a voice that is far too loud for so small a space. He sets all of the mail on a small table near the front door except for a single, invitation sized envelope.

Karl, who silently groans at the disruption of his peaceful reverie, declines to return the greeting.

"You got something here, Karl," Wally announces in a booming voice. And, without waiting for permission to do so, tears open the envelope and reads its contents.

"Oh, my, that's interesting. It's an invitation from your dear Aunt B. Says it's a family reunion down in Oxford, Mississippi."

Although Karl grew up in Oxford, he has almost no recollection of his time there, and doesn't recall an Aunt B.

"Not interested."

"At least look at it," Wally protests, holding the elegant hand-written invitation out to him. "You should go. Do you a world of good. Get out, see people, have fun!"

Karl takes the invitation reluctantly and examines it, looking for some evidence of fraud or artifice, distrustful, mostly because he's unsure which imaginary persona Wally has chosen to adopt for the occasion, still uneasy about the imposter who stood in Wally's place in the church courtyard.

"Come now, it's your dear Aunt B. Read what she says. The poor dear is dying to see you, as are your other aunts, uncles, and cousins. Who knows, Tereza might even show up."

"Tereza?"

"Well, you once said your families were close. She grew up there, didn't she?"

Karl doesn't recall ever telling Wally any such thing. But buried in his mind is a fleeting childhood memory of him and Tereza, playing tag among towering Magnolia trees in some park-like setting, a great house with a large front portico, Corinthian columns and cast-iron balconies. His childhood home? Tereza's home? But no sooner does the image arise than it falls away into obscurity. That fleeting image is enough to convince him that he must accept the invitation.

Wally drones on until Karl holds up a hand to silence him.

"Alright. I'll go."

"Course, you'll go," Wally huffs.

So, on the appointed day, he leaves early for the train station, afraid that he'll arrive late, or not at all. Once there, he sees with relief that the doors to the train platform have been left open.

I'm there, of course, disguised as a porter, rushing ahead of Karl and making sure that no door will impede Karl's progress. He brushes past, without taking notice of me.

As he wanders through the Oxford bound train, searching for the least occupied car, he sees himself seated by the window, quietly reading a newspaper, the Alexandria Times, as it happens.

How does he know it is he? He considers the proposition. He realizes that what he sees is, incontrovertibly and without a shadow of doubt, his body double. Over time, he has come to accept the existence of such body doubles. But that, for Karl, does not put an end to the question.

Do I and this body double, he wonders, share a single consciousness? Or is the replication of my body a simple biological accident? When a body is replicated, does it share consciousness with the life form it replicates? Is the other passenger before whom I have stopped, my actual self, or some other self? He not only resembles me but is dressed exactly the same, right down to the shoelaces.

He continues to stare at the stranger on the train, marveling at the resemblances between him and 'The Other'.

I, too, am breathless with shock and surprise, at once again observing the interaction between body doubles. I'm seated at the far end of the nearly empty car, peeking over a counterfeit passenger manifest which covers most of my face, so I can observe the unfolding scene undetected.

"Karl," he calls out to the train passenger over whom he's been obsessing. He's unsure whether a body double would necessarily be called by the same name as he. He quickly decides this body double is unlikely to be called Karl almost as soon as he's called out the name.

Just as Karl, and I, for that matter, surmised, he, 'The Other', does not respond. Karl, and to be honest, I, as well, opt to use the impersonal title 'The Other' when referring to these body doubles, at least until the question of shared consciousness is resolved.

The Other glances up from his reading with a look of one who has been disturbed without good cause by someone unfamiliar, or peculiar, or even worse.

Karl turns away as The Other, obviously unwilling to engage with him, shakes out his newspaper as though shaking out an unwanted contaminant, a flea or a pest, from its pages. Karl takes a seat far enough away not to be a nuisance, but close enough to observe The Other.

The train rolls along, and Karl falls to speculating whether he and The Other are having the same thoughts, and other such riddles. Does he know Tereza or Wally the Walrus? He cannot rule out the possibility that even if they share a single consciousness, they may well entertain different dreams, memories, and thoughts at any given moment in time.

Did Plutarch, he wonders, refer to the lives of the great men of the ancient world as parallel in the figurative or in the literal sense? Perhaps Pompey and Agesilaus were the same man after all. Or, more likely, they were mere fictions of an overzealous historian, himself implausibly imagined by some anonymous medieval scribe, to whom I feel I must claim some affinity.

Karl must have dozed off and opens his eyes with a start to find The Other standing over him; and looking into his face intently.

"Are you and I the same person?" The Other asks, his voice trembling. "I have this eerie sense that you and I are the same man."

"I believe so, old chum," Karl replies, "but I can neither prove nor disprove the point without some convincing evidence on the issue."

He doesn't know why it occurs to him to refer to The Other as old chum, since, as far as he knows, he's never inhabited the playing fields at Oxford—Oxford, England, that is, not Oxford, Mississippi.

The train rocks and sways along through the lush countryside as he and The Other sit at the edge of their benches facing one another.

The Other breathes a sigh of relief and settles into his back cushion. "I'm called X, by the way," he mumbles.

How appropriate, Karl muses, considering the abundance of alphabetically designated members from whom I receive greetings from time to time, and of whom I have no recollection. But he can't resist the urge to probe deeper.

"X? That's your name?"

"It's what I'm called. My name is Xavier, but no one knows me by that name. You may call me either."

At this point something quite unexpected occurs. I find that I, without any special effort, am able to read Xavier's mind. The voices in his head—which I at first believed were the voices of the people scattered throughout the train—grow more and more intelligible to me with each sentence X utters. I'm quite astounded, as I follow both the voiced and unvoiced colloquy between Karl and his double. This phenomenon, more than any other, convinces me that he and Karl are true doubles with a shared consciousness.

In the meantime, Karl and his double have fallen silent, each deeply pondering the peculiar and untoward situation they now find themselves in. Although obvious to me, Karl is still wondering if they share a single conscious mind and decides to probe further.

"Do you know about the doors?" Karl asks.

If The Other has a door phobia, Karl's thinking, then I have proof that we are true doubles, in both body and mind, and not just mere body doubles.

"Doors? What about them?"

"I gather from your expression that you know nothing of the doors. My therapist says that doors are universal signifiers, that doors…."

"Stuff and nonsense," Xavier mutters, looking around and moving to the edge of his seat as though he's about to depart as suddenly as he appeared.

I'm surprised, Karl muses, that he has disclaimed knowledge of the anomaly of the doors since he and I are one, and therefore my experiences should be his, and his, mine. Perhaps we aren't true doubles after all.

"I myself," Xavier offers, having chosen not to flee, "have never encountered any such preposterous doors. But I must tell you, in all confidence, that when I go to sleep, I sometimes have out of body experiences. The thing is, old man, that I'm not always sure that I shall return to the same body."

Old man, old chum. It's as though Karl and Xavier are two minor characters trapped on a train in some disremembered British comedy from the last century. Sitting at the back of the train car, I cover my mouth to suppress a laugh.

After a moment of embarrassed silence, Xavier continues.

"I haven't slept for weeks from the anxiety attached to this fear of never returning to the same body."

The beads of sweat which appear on Xavier's forehead reveal the fear and dread percolating below the surface of his otherwise passive narration of his out of body experiences.

"The last time," he bravely continues, "I went through several different states: land surveyor, croupier, engineer, and postman."

Karl watches him closely, suspended between indulgent credence and fulsome indifference. He can't help thinking that what he's saying makes absolutely no sense.

How, Karl asks himself, does he know that he has returned to himself? Maybe he is nothing more than a land surveyor, or a croupier, or an engineer, or a postman. He's tempted to ask him, Who, then is the real Xavier? But he keeps his doubts, including his doubts over the supposed continuity of consciousness, to himself as Xavier continues his lament.

"Some states of being," he continues, "have no name. In some cases, I'm utterly invisible, without physical substance, without weight. My existence is unbearably light!" he wails.

Karl tries to console him, carefully and tactfully explaining the blighted nature of human existence, though with little success. He simply hasn't the heart to tell him bluntly that unbearable lightness is its natural condition. So why make such a fuss over it?

He looks at Karl, Karl looks at him, then they stare, for a time, at their hazy images reflected on the window glass looking like two drowning men. In unison, they exhale loudly, relaxing slightly. To lighten the somber mood of their colloquy, Karl asks him where he's bound.

Xavier replies that he's returning to Alexandria, Virginia, after a visit with Tereza's family in Oxford, Mississippi.

Karl's surprised that he's mentioned Tereza, and is about to press him for details when another question takes hold of his consciousness.

"Did you say you're returning to Alexandria?"

"Trains only have one destination at a time, old chum," Xavier replies grinning, "and it's either Oxford at one terminus, or Alexandria at the other."

"I'm afraid you're on the wrong train, old boy. This train is bound for Oxford, having originated several hours ago at Alexandria."

"Oh, no, I'm afraid you're quite mistaken. I only just boarded this train at the station outside of Oxford not more than four hours ago," he explains, examining his fob watch.

"Well, one of us has got it wrong, or perhaps we are both right," Karl replies.

"Or perhaps we have both got it wrong, ha, ha," he says, thrusting that repugnant finger, his middle finger, into Karl's chest a bit too forcefully, without tact, as one might assault an antagonist against whom one feels nothing but contempt.

"Ah hah, but it is neither here nor there, some trick of Time and Space, old boy." Karl is aware that the acid is not withheld from his voice as he thrusts his chest forward, slapping his odious finger away.

Karl and Xavier are both aware, it turns out, that each is contemplating the exchange of blows. But each dismisses the thought of fisticuffs at the same moment, instead exchanging forced smiles. There's a prolonged lull in their colloquy, and they begin to look around the train car, trying to avoid one another's gaze.

"By the way, Karl asks, hoping to break the bleak mood that engulfs them, how was your visit with Tereza?"

"Oh, yes, ha, ha," he replies with an embarrassed laugh, "I never saw her. Her cousin Tamar told me she'd just left in some haste back to her hideaway in Alexandria. That's why I'm heading back there today."

His response makes no sense, of course, but Karl doesn't want to provoke another dispute about the train's destination. He sits in sullen silence for a moment, deciding his next move.

But the strain of meeting his double and the monotonous rhythm of the lumbering train conspire to deaden Karl's senses, even as he continues to gaze at his double.

Xavier begins to fade and blur and is gone forever in the early morning light.

Did he cease to exist for me, Karl wonders as he succumbs to a deep sleep, or I for him?

Waking again with a start, he hears the conductor announce the train's arrival at a small city outside of Oxford.

Still disoriented from the recent encounter with himself, he leaves the station in search of a cab. I follow at a discreet distance, but close enough so that I can still tune in to his thoughts.

He enters a hired car, a convertible with its top down, and instructs the driver, an extremely aged gentleman, to take him to such and such an address. I step into another car.

"Follow that car!" I instruct the driver, pointing in Karl's direction.

Not far behind him, I watch as the driver of Karl's car peers at him quizzically over wire rimmed pince-nez, then, after a short trip the car stops in front of the Oxford City Library. Karl checks the invitation from his Aunt B and finds that the ancient gentleman has indeed taken him to the correct address.

When he asks the driver about his family, he replies that he has lived in Oxford all his life, and that although he knows of the family, he believes they all perished in the Great Flood of '04, without specifying the century.

Oddly relieved by the belated news of his family's demise, he instructs the driver to return him to the station where, without uttering a single word to another soul, he boards the train for Alexandria. Still dressed in my porter's uniform, I go ahead of Karl to ensure that all the doors are open to him.

Upon searching the seat he had occupied, and well after he left the train car and made his way into the Alexandria station, I found his summary of the return trip, in his own hand, scribbled on a discarded napkin.

"It's been a relaxing journey home," he wrote, "except that a peculiar looking gentleman has had the impertinence to stare at me for the entire return journey home."

No matter how often I've puzzled over Karl's cryptic description of his return to Alexandria, its meaning continues to elude me, as does the anomaly of a single train traveling in two different directions at the same time, arriving and departing at the same moment.

Nine

What follows is a narration of the colloquy between Karl and Wally in Karl's apartment. How do I know who said what to whom? Like any good spy, I have my sources and methods; and like any good spy, I am not free to divulge them. Or, if you wish, you may simply assume that I have invented this exchange between them from whole cloth.

Karl, who has just entered those private precincts, peers into the living room and sees that Wally the Walrus is seated in one of two large leather armchairs, absorbed in his work, slowly deciphering the stick figures stamped on a large clay tablet, pausing from time to time to scribble in his notepad or to lift a large glass of amber liquid to his swollen lips. His enormous body so consumes the chair that it's scarcely visible under his bulk.

Wally, who has not yet acknowledged Karl, continues his work. As he gazes at him, Karl imagines a large sea creature reclining upon an unseaworthy barge, listing slothfully in the oil slick waters of some unmemorable back bay, its untended canvas flapping loose to the winds, its prow swamped in an alcoholic flood.

While Karl wonders whether Wally is imaginary, he knows that Wally isn't imaginary in any commonly accepted sense of the word. Rather, in Karl's mind, Wally is imaginary in the sense that he imagines himself to be this or that, depending on the circumstances. By the same logic, Karl believes both he and Wally exist in the imagination of each; that he, Karl, is a figment of Wally's imagination just as Wally is a figment of Karl's.

The more Karl ponders the point, the more he becomes hopelessly lost in the labyrinth of language. He's almost grateful when The Walrus intrudes into his ever more confused thoughts.

"Ah!" Wally exclaims, suddenly alerted to Karl's presence. "Come, Theodore, sit," he gushes, putting aside the heavy clay tablet and rising from his chair. Not an easy task, considering the energy required to move such a mass of protoplasm.

Karl moves cautiously into the room, increasingly wary of his imaginary friend's words and actions, especially since Karl never uses the name Theodore, his nom-de-plume. He's debating whether to correct Wally when Wally interrupts his thoughts.

"I'm working on a new play," Wally announces as he makes for the kitchen next to the living room. Once there, he takes two glasses from a cupboard and fills them with whiskey. He knows exactly where everything is, as though he's lived there for ages.

Perhaps he has lived here for ages, Karl thinks, and it is I who am the interloper. Karl imagines himself an itinerant, moving from shelter to shelter, with no direction home, but rejects the image as unsavory.

Wally returns, hands Karl a full glass of whiskey, and settles down in the easy chair, crushing it with his bulk once again into the shape of a flat river barge.

"Well, aren't you going to say something? About my new play?"

"Is that cuneiform?" Karl asks, pointing to the tablet Wally has propped up against the wall, alongside a cluster of dusty, broken clay tablets.

"Research, my boy. Can't write a play about love, the soul, numerology, or dying, for that matter, without reference to the Hittites."

"Hittites?"

"Greatest civilization that ever existed, knew everything about everything. I've never written a play without some reference to the Hittites."

"What's this play about?"

"It's called Dead Souls."

"That story's already been written."

"Ha, ha, very funny. But this is a serious work about people who bargain away their souls. We're not talking about Russian peasants, by Jove! These are Hittites, noblest race of humans that ever lived. But still, there were those among them that didn't die, see, they just went on living without a soul. Hittites wrote about them. Not many people know about Hittite letters and science. Most people don't care a damn about 'em."

"Count me among them."

Wally ignores the jibe, and thoughtfully takes a slow and measured sip from his glass, like an aging and honorably wounded British Light Colonel about to recount his travails in the Crimean War, without specifying the century, his bushy brows scrunched massively over his drooping eyelids.

They sit in silence, and Karl begins to slip into a meditative state, abetted by copious amounts of whiskey too quickly consumed. But his reverie is broken abruptly.

"Now your Hittites had six fingers on each hand," Wally announces in a stentorian voice, as if resuming a long lost lecture; now an absent minded professor, freshly retired after a long and distinguished military career and into Academe, tutoring an anxious clutch of undergraduates thirsty for sex, adventure and knowledge, precisely in that order, even if vicarious.

For his part, Karl is barely attentive, having dismissed the chosen topic as ludicrous. "Six fingers, indeed!" he mutters.

"That, of course," Wally drones on, "explains why the Hittite's number system was based on twelve, while we, with fewer digits, enjoy a number system based on ten." He pauses for dramatic effect.

"Hittites. Hah!" he exclaims, emitting a deep throated chuckle which causes a wave of flesh to ripple down his enormous body, from his inflamed and bulging cheeks to his gelatinous belly. Santa Claus on lysergic acid, Miguel de Unamuno on phencyclidine, Aldous Huxley on mescaline, with his arms wrapped around William Blake, the two of them sobbing with homoerotic joy, euphoric because they've pierced the doors of perception, the same doors, presumably, of which Carl Jung sang, the doors of perception which inspire nothing in Karl but naked fear, labored breathing and nervous tremors.

"I'm waiting for you to explain what the Hittites have to do with this new play of yours."

"Thought you'd never ask," says Wally, animated at his companion's unexpected display of interest. He rises from his comfortable chair and rummages through the clay tablets resting against a nearby wall. He selects one, lifts it with both hands over his head, imitating Rembrandt's Moses with the Ten Commandments, and carries it toward the hearth.

"Says right here," he says, gently setting the tablet on the fireplace mantel, "that the Hittites believed in the transmigration of souls. They weighed their dead immediately before, and immediately after death. The difference in weight, in their opinion, must be attributed to the soul. Those whose corpses weighed less after death were great souls, the difference in weight attributed to the transmigration of the deceased person's soul onto some higher plane of self-realization. Those great souls were accorded full funereal honors, streets and public spaces named after them, and their statutes erected in the pantheon."

"I don't see how this fits into your play," Karl says.

"Well of course you don't. I haven't got to the good part yet. What the Hittites figured out from their study of migrating souls is that most of the living walk around with dead souls inside of them. Hittites called it 'unbearable lightness.' Now, everyone knows that a good necromancer can communicate with dead souls. But only a Hittite necromancer was able to restore a dead soul to life. All he needed was a willing donor, one of those folks walking around with a dead soul inside. The donor would get his silver ingots, the Hittite necromancer would get the donor's soul, he'd put it in a bottle, and sell it to rich folks who needed more weight on their souls to receive burial honors. Course, you might need up to ten dead souls to make some measurable weight. But those old Hittite boys knew how to do it all."

"And that's your play?"

"Here, read it for yourself." He hands the manuscript to Karl. "I'm leaving."

Karl hears Wally descending the front steps of the apartment leading to the red brick sidewalk below. Alone at last, Karl enjoys the cozy solace and silence of his sitting room. The firelight from the hearth dwindles into a mere whisper of embers. He picks up the manuscript resting on his lap, and, taken by a sudden curiosity, turns on the lamps and begins to read.

The main protagonist, who is in love with an unnamed woman, is himself never named in the script. Instead, the number 1 is assigned to his speeches. He's described as a heavily bearded middle-aged man of stocky build and swarthy complexion suggesting Mediterranean origins.

In the first act, character number 1 discovers that he shares his soul with multiple doubles, a phenomenon which causes him great anxiety, and interferes with his desire to wed his beloved. He becomes friends with a very large gentleman, identified as number 2, who is described as an itinerant twelve-fingered necromancer. He stops when he reads the following dialog from the second act, his mind in turmoil, unwilling to go on.

Number 2: Your pain is great because your soul is divided. It stands in the way of the marital happiness you seek with the woman you love. For, how can a man with a divided soul bare his soul to his betrothed when that soul is shared by so many others? How can such a man stop those who share his soul from sharing the joy which should be his alone?

Number 1: Tell me, please, I can't live without Number 3 [his beloved]! What must I do to end this torment?

Number 2: You must surrender your soul to me. I shall capture the souls of your doubles and unite them with yours. I shall restore to your body an undivided soul. Only then can you enjoy the fruits of a perfect union with an undivided and unencumbered soul.

Number 1: Oh yes, yes, at once! I surrender my soul and place my body in your hands!

Karl puts down the manuscript, taken by a sudden sense of doom. His first thought is that it is wise to be wary of Wally. He then begins to wonder what part Wally might play in his continuing failure to possess Tereza. The more Karl considers these possibilities, the more convinced he is that Wally is a dangerous rival.

I, of course, reached the same conclusion some time ago. For that reason I began of late to follow Wally on his nocturnal peregrinations through the darkest streets of Alexandria. I've observed that he tends to associate with unsavory looking characters from the underworld. While his movements are certainly suspicious, I haven't yet discerned in them any nefarious scheme aimed at bringing Karl to ruin.

Ten

At a riverfront café in Alexandria, one of his favorite haunts, Karl sits, waiting for the waiter to return with the latest edition of the Times. His mind, too exhausted to continue deliberations about how best to respond to the potential threat posed by Wally the Walrus, enjoys a moment of repose.

The waiter, Jeremiah, familiar with his habits, doesn't wait for Karl to bid him to retrieve his coffee and the latest edition of his beloved Times. Jeremiah scurries off on that errand as soon as he catches sight of his master.

Karl is gazing at the rushing waters of the Potomac when a well-dressed man has the impertinence to approach his table and casually pulls a chair out for himself.

"Do you mind?" the stranger asks, nonchalantly, then sits without waiting for a response.

He looks to Karl like a banker, shiny, buttered hair neatly parted, wire rim glasses, the cuffs of his starched white shirt adorned with silver links. His appearance is in stark contrast to Karl's disheveled hair, his unruly beard, and rumpled clothes.

"I know you," the banker says.

I, who am seated at the far end of the patio, become aware that I heard the banker's words before he uttered them. As for Karl, I know from his thoughts that it hasn't yet occurred to him that he's in the presence of yet another double. Instead, he's convinced that the banker is another bothersome fan.

"No, not just another fan," the banker comments.

Has he read my thoughts? Karl wonders.

"Yes," the banker replies, "I have read your thoughts."

"I'm quite sure you cannot possibly have read my thoughts," Karl protests.

"It's quite simple, we're the same person. No, you needn't insist. I will go away if you wish."

He's guessed that Karl was about to insist that he leave, but then another thought pops into Karl's head.

"And now," the imposter announces, "you're thinking, how can two bodies, so unlike in appearance, sitting in two different chairs, be one person? And that question intrigues you, am I right?"

He has again guessed the question exactly as Karl framed it in his head.

"Begin," says the imposter, "with the proposition that consciousness is simply fragmented. There are times, when we are anesthetized, or when our minds go blank, for example, during which our consciousness, and our self-awareness with it, is suspended. Where does our mind go?"

"Yes," Karl replies, borrowing the imposter's thoughts, "it is possible that fragments of what we think of as our consciousness may be dispersed indiscriminately over time and space. Then…."

"Then," says the imposter, continuing Karl's thoughts, "it's just a matter of simple probabilities."

"Yes," Karl adds, "but what are the chances that I should encounter a fragment of my consciousness here, in this space, at this time? I might as well guess the chances of double fives appearing on five successive rolls of the dice."

"Exactly," says the imposter, putting a reassuring hand on Karl's shoulder, a broad smile creasing his eyelids and warping his lips.

Just then Jeremiah the waiter, Arthur's look-alike, returns with a copy of the Times for Karl and the cup of coffee that he knows Karl craves.

"Your newspaper, sir." Then, to the imposter, "something for monsieur?"

"Yes, I'll have what this gentleman is having," the banker replies, pointing to Karl's coffee.

"Very good, monsieur."

Jeremiah is about to turn away when the imposter addresses him.

"Wait, I have a question for you."

"Very well," answers Jeremiah, affably.

"Would you say that I and this bearded gentleman resemble one another?"

"Ha, ha, ha" laughs Jeremiah, "you're joking, sir. I've never seen two such dissimilar looking men in my entire life."

Karl stares at the banker, reading his mind. He knows the banker asked that question to demonstrate that true doubles need not resemble one another.

It's a possibility that I, too, never anticipated, but, faced with this empirical evidence, it's a possibility I now readily admit to.

"Hmm, yes, quite right," responds the banker. He smiles and winks at Karl, then turns to Jeremiah.

"Let me put another question to you then, if I may. Have you ever encountered your double?"

"Double?" asks Jeremiah, puzzled.

"Yes, your exact double, someone identical to you, who thinks and perhaps even looks like you?"

"Well," Jeremiah replies, grinning, "I've heard stories of such doubles, but I doubt that such things exist."

What Jeremiah is thinking, but does not mention, is about the similarity between himself and Arthur, the waiter at Chez Albert, so alike in appearance, speech, mannerisms, and thoughts that even intimates confuse one for the other.

"But, just imagine," continues the imposter, "that one fine day you run into your double. Then what?"

"I suppose I would have to kill him," Jeremiah answers with a forced chuckle. After a short hesitation his mind is, no doubt, working through the possibility that Arthur is more than just a look-alike, and the prospect of murdering him conjures thoughts and images he has hitherto managed to suppress. The smile disappears from his face.

"Assassin!" Jeremiah cries out as if he were just then imagining himself hacking poor Arthur into bloody pieces. His body convulses, jerking this way and that, as if struggling to cast out some demon.

It's obvious to Karl, to his uninvited guest, and to all the patrons of that small, insignificant riverfront café, who've suddenly turned their attention upon the trio of interlocutors, that Jeremiah is struggling with some grave internal conflict.

Then, as if wakening from a deep slumber, Jeremiah's body shakes itself, he opens his eyes, he smiles, he laughs, he sings, he dances around the tables, a veritable Petrouchka, his apron fanning out like a ballerina's tutu as he executes multiple plié and jeté to the applause of all the patrons who've been gazing upon the unfolding scene, at first with consternation, but now with delight and admiration.

The performance goes on for several minutes as Jeremiah flies from one end of the patio to the other. But the gaiety ends as abruptly as it began. Jeremiah displays another sudden shift in mood. He stares at the table where Karl and the imposter/banker are still seated and cautiously approaches. He stops when he reaches Karl's side and stares at him.

I, who have been observing the unfolding scene, have tried in vain to penetrate Jeremiah's mind. While I don't succeed in reading his thoughts, it's clear to me that it has suddenly occurred to Jeremiah that Karl and the banker may themselves be doubles, despite their different appearances.

I note, as well, that the banker, whose mind is open to me, has been watching Karl closely for some reaction, not to Jeremiah's impromptu performance, but rather to Jeremiah's pronouncement that one should not hesitate to annihilate one's double in the event of an encounter.

When Karl fails to react, Jeremiah slinks off into the interior of the café, as if hiding from some public embarrassment. By this time the on-lookers have lost interest in Jeremiah's antics, and resume their inane conversations in hushed tones, like an audience after the entertainment ends, the curtain has fallen, and the performers have left the stage.

Although Jeremiah returned to the kitchen inside the café, presumably to fetch the coffee the imposter had requested, he never does so.

The imposter/banker and Karl sit quietly across from one another, trying to avoid eye contact. They're both thinking about what Jeremiah said about destroying his double, although Karl can tell from the imposter's thoughts, just as the imposter can tell from Karl's, that neither desires to destroy the other.

"At least, not at this moment," both the imposter and Karl say at the same time, each to the other. They smile at one another as though chagrined by so glaring an admission that each has, in fact, considered the annihilation of the other, if only for a fleeting moment. Then they fall silent.

A question about the imposter leaps into Karl's head, seemingly from nowhere, which the imposter promptly answers.

"I'm called Z," he says, answering Karl's unvoiced question, "after Y, the twenty-sixth letter of the alphabet; but...."

"Your name is Zeke," Karl says, completing Z's thought. "What...."

"Do I do for a living?" Zeke asks, finishing Karl's question.

"Don't tell me," Karl retorts, "you're an actor, currently auditioning..., wait, don't tell me..., for a part in a play called Dead Souls?"

"This is ludicrous," the banker says, frowning. "How can we carry on a conversation when you know what I'm thinking, and I know what you're thinking?"

"Exactly. And now you're thinking about…,"

"Tereza and Wally…,

"And the…,

"Doors. Yes, the accursed doors," Z says.

"You're thinking about Dr. Sax and his strange methods."

"Voodoo is what it is. I'll never…,"

"Return?"

"I'm sorry, I can't…,"

"I know, neither can I. It's futile to attempt conversation. We need only read our own minds…"

The silence which descends is interrupted by Jeremiah's approach. Karl watches Jeremiah as he emerges from the café's interior toward him in slow motion, somewhat relieved by the distraction, feeling mentally exhausted by his efforts to untangle the banker's thoughts from his own.

I, too, still watching from the far end of the patio, feel some mental fatigue. Then the strangest thing happens, the world goes topsy-turvy.

Time slows, then stands still. Birds' flights are arrested in midair. The currents of the river below cease to rush. Deep silence descends. Then….

The wheel of seasons spins. From bright green, the leaves of all the nearby trees turn red and yellow and tumble to the ground, snow falls, freezes, then melts, rain comes in torrents, then in warm sheets. Stars collide in the Void, black holes swirl and new born stars shimmer. The sun plummets from the sky, the light vanishes from the heavens, darkness descends, stars rise, poppies spread over sainted ground, cadavers molder in dark, moist soil. The Angel Gabriel blows into his horn. But it makes not a sound.

Patrons come and go, quickly, noiselessly, as in a time-lapsed video.

Then, just as suddenly the skies lighten, clouds roam aimlessly, the river's waters gush noisily, birds take wing, crying loudly, in protest to what, no one can say.

Although I witnessed the entire cataclysm, I couldn't say how many suns rose or seasons passed. Neither I nor Karl know.

Then, at last, Jeremiah arrives at his table.

"May I bring you anything else, Monsieur Karl?" Jeremiah asks.

"What about my friend's coffee?" he asks, pointing to the now vacant chair the imposter, who was called Z, had occupied.

"What friend?" Jeremiah asks, looking around.

Eleven

Karl is strolling down the crowded boulevard, out for a walk just before sunset. From out of nowhere, a stranger sidles up to him and whispers in his ear.

"I have a message for you."

"Go away," Karl says, angry at being accosted by a total stranger. But the stranger keeps abreast of him, leans in and whispers again into his ear.

"Tereza is at the Cecil Hotel."

Karl stops dead in his tracks and turns toward the stranger's voice to demand more information. But the stranger is nowhere to be seen. Bewildered, Karl has difficulty thinking straight. He resolves to run in search of Tereza, whom he hasn't seen, or heard, or touched, or kissed in an eternity. He pushes through the crowds, running in the direction of the hotel.

I'm forced to decide between chasing after the anonymous messenger and following Karl. Tracking that stranger might provide clues concerning what seems to be a nefarious plot against Karl, and might even lead to the mastermind behind it.

But then, what if Karl is running headlong into some dangerous trap? My responsibility is clear. I chase after him until I find him standing outside the hotel's open doors.

When he enters the hotel in search of Tereza, he's informed by the desk clerk that Tereza is not a guest. He protests, raising his voice, arguing with the hotel staff until the futility of his efforts becomes clear. Still hopeful, despite a growing suspicion that he has been duped, he takes a seat in the lobby, watching a parade of guests enter and depart.

Hours later, convinced that he has been duped, he leaves the hotel. He can't help wondering who is behind this hoax, but comes back to the same answer. It must be Wally the Walrus's doing. But why? And how to prove it?

Karl moves aimlessly down the boulevard, struggling with his suspicions, with his anger, with his disappointments. Before long he finds himself outside Chez Albert. He stops to peer through the restaurant windows, trying to decide whether to drop in for a bite to eat. It's late. And he's hungry, not having eaten a proper meal since the day before yesterday.

Through the glass, he scans the large dining room and catches sight of Tereza sitting alone at a table. She looks toward the window in Karl's direction, smiling, and, with elegant movements of arm, wrist and hand, sets a pearl cigarette holder with the delicate fingers of her gloved hand down upon a glass ashtray next to a half empty cocktail glass.

Is it really her? he wonders.

He catches the waiter's eye, and points to the closed restaurant door, fortunate that it happens to be Arthur, the head waiter, who knows Karl and of his fear of closed doors. He scurries to the door and greets him with open arms.

"Bon soir, monsieur, ce fait long temps, mon ami! Do you know who is dining with us tonight?" he asks, excitedly. "It's Tereza! You and she used to dine here regularly. Before the unfortunate events...."

"Yes," Karl replies, cutting him off. "I saw her through the window as I was passing by."

"This way, monsieur."

I slip quietly into the restaurant after Karl and find a place at the restaurant's bar, situated in a nook adjacent to the entrance, where I can covertly surveille Karl as he makes his way through the large dining room.

Everyone's staring at them as Arthur takes his hand and leads him toward Tereza's table. As Karl traverses the immense dining hall, he drops Arthur's hand, stopping to gaze at a mural covering almost the entire wall. It depicts the Stranger, Meursault, being led to the guillotine, surrounded by an excited, cheering throng of blood-thirsty spectators.

He's often viewed this painting and knows it by heart. Of course, he's always noticed that the Meursault of the mural resembles him so closely that it could well be a mirror image. But this time, as he gazes at the painting, he also sees, for the very first time, that the executioner looks just like Wally the Walrus.

Arthur tugs at his arm, and he turns away from the mural, gulping down his anxiety, moving through the crowded restaurant, trying to ignore the excited, cheerful faces seated at every table who stare up at him, as if he, himself, were being led to the guillotine.

He arrives at Tereza's table at last, Arthur pulling out a chair for him, smiling broadly, delighted that he and his Tereza are reunited at last.

"Tereza?" Karl says tentatively. He hasn't yet taken the seat offered by Arthur, and hovers near her, awaiting some sign of recognition, unsure how he will be received.

She looks up, startled, then leaps from her chair, moves quickly toward him and, inches from his face, reels back and delivers a stinging blow with an open hand to his cheek with such force that his head snaps back causing him nearly to lose his balance.

"You bastard!" she cries out.

Were it not for Arthur's quick reactions, Karl would certainly have fallen. A reddish welt glows on his cheek from which beads of blood are leaking.

Karl is too stunned to speak. Arthur, who is still nearby, looks bewildered, and discreetly backs away from the table.

"How dare you show your face after the way you've treated me! You bastard!" she repeats in a noticeably Eastern European accent, as her tears begin to flow. She collapses into her chair and puts her hands over her face, sobbing.

All the restaurant patrons are staring at Tereza and Karl, some are standing for a better view of the unfolding scene; some are using their cell phone cameras to video the drama.

"Tereza, please, I can explain everything…," Karl says at last.

"Don't you dare speak! When you left me there at the altar, I hoped never to see your face again. Just go away!"

"I will go if you wish. But you should know that I did not leave you at the altar of my own free will. If you'll just hear me out…."

"There's nothing more to be said. You rejected me in the cruelest way. Nothing you can say will change that."

A murmur runs through the crowd, and people are now pointing at Karl. Their murmuring grows louder and Tereza turns toward them to see what the commotion is about. She notices that a man at the nearest table is repeatedly pointing to his cheek and then pointing to Karl.

"For God's sake, Madam, look what you've done!" several patrons call out simultaneously.

She looks over at Karl.

"You're bleeding!"

"Bleeding? Me?"

"Did I do that? Your cheek.... I'm so sorry…."

She turns to Arthur.

"Don't just stand there! Go get a bandage or something to stop the bleeding."

Arthur scurries off to the kitchen for a first aid kit. In the meantime she dips her cloth napkin into a glass of ice water, wiping away the blood which by now has reached his chin, then presses the cold napkin against his cheek, holding his head in the crook of her arm.

"Poor Karl, I never meant to hurt you in this way."

"You did," says Arthur returning with the first aid kit.

"Yes, you did," a chorus of anonymous patrons echo. A murmur of agreement runs through the dining hall.

"Well maybe I did," Tereza confesses, facing the crowd.

"But he deserved it!" an anonymous woman shouts out.

"No," Arthur says, "he didn't."

"You are a peculiar fellow, aren't you?" Tereza says, looking angrily at Arthur.

"Yes, madam, I am a peculiar fellow," he replies. "But in this instance, I am right and you are wrong. And if you allow Karl to speak you will certainly agree."

"Well said!" a gentleman calls out from his table.

"Let the man talk!" a woman at another table shouts, and the crowd begins to chant, "Let the man talk!" stamping their feet, whistling, and clapping.

"Do you wish to tell me something?" Tereza asks, bringing the crowd's chanting and hooting to an abrupt end. She looks at Karl with scorn.

"May I?" He moves his chair closer to Tereza's until their shoulders touch.

"I have wronged you, Tereza. Please forgive me. I will never abandon you in the future ever again."

They kiss. All the restaurant patrons who are still on their feet, applaud, cheer, and whistle in approval. They come up to the table one by one to shake the happy couple's hands, then return to their tables, retrieve their belongings and exit the restaurant.

I, too, leave Chez Albert, satisfied that the lovers have reconciled, and that the scene has ended on a high note.

Twelve

Later, how much later Karl cannot say, but later, he and Tereza stand together in the darkened entry way of his apartment locked in a passionate embrace. In a frenzy, they begin to tear at one another's garments. Nearly naked, they make for the bedroom and tumble onto his bed.

He pleasures her all night.

Then, in the morning, wrapped in an embrace, they vow never to lose touch again. Tereza gives Karl the address of her apartment in Alexandria.

"Why have you never told me that you have an apartment in Alexandria?"

"Oh, it's not really my place. It belongs to a friend. Besides, I'm rarely there, now that I'm in rehearsals for a new play off Broadway. I just use it as a maildrop and for storage. Besides, your door is always open, so I'll drop in whenever I'm in town. Now I really must be on my way," she tells him, getting out of bed and searching for her clothes. "I have a train to catch."

"Why don't you move in with me? We could live together. And maybe… maybe we can still get married."

She doesn't respond.

"Tereza, will you marry me?"

"Never."

I watch Tereza walk out of Karl's open front door to an awaiting car. What Karl doesn't know is that the title of the play Tereza is to appear in is Dead Souls.

I know about Tereza's role in Dead Souls from having followed Wally to rehearsals at a small theater and have seen all the cast members there, including Tereza, Zeke, and Xavier. Something like a devious scheme is starting to take shape in my head which I'm struggling to piece together into a full-blown plot.

Thirteen

Karl walks down the narrow hallway connecting his apartment's open front door to the bedrooms at the rear of the apartment. He gazes into the hallway mirror. There's an image reflected in the mirror, and he stares at it, trying to recollect whom it most resembles.

He raises his left arm. The image raises its right arm. Upon such proofs he decides, at last, that it must be his own image, now restored to its proper place in time and space.

"Thank you," he and his mirror image say, although the voice of his image is delayed by a milli-second. Bothered by the delayed response, he looks back into the glass and finds that his image has disappeared.

He groans in despair.

I know many of the events I've set down strain credulity. I, too, struggle with their utter implausibility. If I may point out, however, they are no less implausible than, to take one example, Immanuel Kant's phenomena and noumena (ding an sich).

Fourteen

The following day, Karl returns to Dr. Sax's suite of offices; this time to consult him regarding the mirrors. To his surprise, all the doors in the good doctor's office have been left open and some of them have been removed completely.

Does the psychotherapist share my door phobia? he wonders. He proceeds, unobstructed, into the therapist's empty waiting room. The entire suite, including his private office, is barren of furniture and furnishings.

He enters the doctor's inner sanctum, also devoid of furnishings, including the life-sized portrait of Carl Jung. He finds Dr. Sax seated on the floor, resting on a short stool with an opium pipe gurgling in front of him.

He stands there, waiting for Dr. Sax to acknowledge his existence. The good doctor has apparently discarded all clothing apparel, even the famous pince-nez is gone.

"Go away," he croaks, like a frog from its toadstool, sensing Karl's presence. "I'm no longer seeing patients. I've abandoned the practice."

"But, but, why?" Karl stammers.

"Too many tiresome patients, too many psychoses. It is far too obvious that madness is not an aberration. I've known this all along, but hoped, in vain, to be mistaken. Madness, far from being an aberration, is the defining feature of the human condition. Those patients I could not euthanize or have committed I've turned away; the remainder are simply untreatable. For this reason, I'm no longer seeing patients."

"I'm sorry," Karl responds. "I was hoping you could help me as you did, so ably, once before."

Dr. Sax looks Karl up and down, curses, then dons his pince-nez, even though it is now obvious, even to Karl, that Dr. Sax is as blind as a bat.

"Very well, then. Stand on your head," he instructs. When Karl hesitates, the doctor explains.

"It's an empirically tested technique, comrade, and an effective diagnostic tool, even for those who've read the Critique of Pure Reason, or Of Grammatology, for that matter."

Karl knows better than to question the good doctor's methods and struggles to stand on his head. After falling in a heap following several attempts, Dr. Sax snorts in disgust.

"Enough!" he exclaims.

"But doctor...," Karl begins to protest. Dr. Sax cuts him off.

"Commotio speculorum," he mumbles. Then, in a bored monotone adds, "You're here about the mirrors."

Once again Karl is speechless, amazed at the therapist's diagnostic powers. He has never mentioned the mirrors to a living soul.

"Mirrors and doors, doors and mirrors," Sax intones. "Noumena and Phenomena."

"What?" Karl is lost, fearing another lecture about universal signifiers, Carl Jung, and Jean Paul Sartre.

"The idols of the tribe are inherent in human nature," Sax continues, "for man's sense is falsely asserted to be the standard of things; on the contrary, all the perceptions both of the senses and the mind bear reference to man and not to the universe, and the human mind resembles those uneven mirrors which impart their own properties to different objects, from which rays are emitted and distort and disfigure them."

"What does that mean?" Karl asks, bewildered.

I listen enthralled, captivated by Sax's recitation of Aphorism 41 from Francis Bacon's Novum Organum, a radical break from an obsolete Aristotelean epistemology. I understand exactly what the good doctor is getting at.

"Mirrors terrify us because they show us the inherent fallibility of human knowledge. The mind is like a mirror which captures only images of things but not the things as they exist in nature, 'ding an sich' as that German pedant used to say. The mirror cannot see itself, and that is **what terrifies us about mirrors because, like a mirror, the conscious mind cannot see itself**!!!!!"

Dr. Sax is screaming as he pronounces these last words and begins to tear at the tuft of hair which nearly circumnavigates his scalp. Then, suddenly, his arms fall to his sides, his head slumps, he begins to snore loudly as his pince-nez slips from his nose and the bamboo stem of his pipe falls to the floor without making a sound.

Karl stands there, waiting for the good doctor to explain. Tired of standing, he lets his body slide down to the floor.

Hours later Dr. Sax finally rouses himself.

"What should I do about the mirrors?" Karl asks hurriedly, before Dr. Sax can slip once again into that starry night of preconscious oblivion.

"The mirrors," Dr. Sax intones, "remove them at once."

Then he nods off, a smile growing on his countenance until it swallows his face.

Karl returns home weary as from a long journey. I stay behind, inspecting Sax's chambers as he sleeps. I'm shocked to find an elegantly bound book in a corner on the floor entitled, 'Toward a Phenomenology of Self' by an anonymous author, which is the title of a monograph I've been working on for the last ten years. The first few pages are enough to convince me that the work is mine.

As for Karl, when he gets home, he takes down all the mirrors, stacking them in a backyard shed where he's stored all the doors he had removed long ago.

While the removal of doors and mirrors from the apartment makes it easier for Karl to move around his apartment, he must still avoid them when he is anywhere else. More importantly, his actions have done nothing to end his fear of further encounters with his doubles.

As for me, I'm outraged that someone has stolen the draft of an opus that is my life's work.

Fifteen

Karl is in his sitting room, scribbling in his notebook. Wally is away, working on producing his play in a distant city, which affords Karl the solitude and silence he craves. Well into the plot of his next novel, his repose is interrupted by a sudden commotion. He looks up and sees Jeremiah and Arthur standing side-by-side at the threshold of his sitting room. He can't, of course, say which is which because of the striking resemblance between them. Both appear battered and beaten, their knuckles red and swollen, lips split, cheeks red and puffy, their eyes blackened.

"Please forgive the intrusion," Jeremiah and Arthur say at the same time.

"Be still," says one man to the other, "let me do the talking."

"I will not," says the second man to the first, "Karl is as much my friend as he is yours. I have every right to speak to him."

They square off, fists clenched. Karl fears that the two will come to blows.

"Gentlemen, gentlemen, please!" he exclaims. "You are both welcome here. But may I know which of you is Jeremiah and which is Arthur?"

"Here," says the first speaker as he plucks a petunia from a nearby floral arrangement and puts it in his hair. "I am Jeremiah, and this miscreant," he points to the man next to him, "is Arthur."

Arthur is about to answer back when Karl interrupts.

"What's happened to you? You both look as though you've suffered a horrific beating. Please sit down, both of you, and tell me what's happened."

They refuse to sit and begin speaking loudly and rapidly trying to drown each other out until Karl, who can't make out what either is saying, raises a hand to still them.

"Please, gentlemen, calm yourselves. Sit down and be still! Here's how we'll proceed. When I point to you, you may speak, and when I show you the palm of my hand you must yield to the other."

When they're seated, Karl points to the petunia adorned Jeremiah. "You first."

"There is a girl, the most beautiful girl in the world, whom I adore. Her name is Matilda, and she loves me. But this oaf," he directs a scornful look at Arthur, "hopes to steal her away from me...."

Karl raises his palm and then points to Arthur.

"Lies! Tillie and I are madly in love and have been sweethearts for ages. Then, this miscreant," he thrusts a finger at Jeremiah, nearly poking him in the eye, "appeared and began to court her, even though he cares nothing for her and does it only to spite me."

"Shut your mouth, you shit eating liar!" shouts Jeremiah.

"Tu te tais! Tu n'es qu'un fils de pute!" shouts Arthur. ["You shut up! You're nothing but a son-of-a-whore!"]

In a sudden rage, they both leap from their chairs, each placing his hands around the other's throat.

"STOP!" shouts Karl, who is also on his feet, struggling to separate them. "This won't do at all. It's no way for civilized men to resolve their differences. I can tell from the intensity of your emotions that both of you are in love with this woman. It's also plain that unless you settle your dispute amicably, you'll end up killing each other." Both of the combatants, again, grudgingly take their seats and nod their heads in agreement.

"You're right, my friend," says Jeremiah. "The fact is we need your help. We can think of no one more suited to this role. It's why we've come to you. We need some way, perhaps a contest of some sort, to determine which of us may rightfully possess Matilda."

"Agreed," says the other. "What about pistols at dawn? You, Karl, could preside over the duel, and set down all of the necessary rules."

"Absolutely out of the question," Karl retorts. "Dueling accomplishes nothing. In the majority of cases it ends, at best, in no more than a near fatal injury, owing to poor marksmanship. Worse yet, it generally leaves both parties disgruntled at the survival of the other, and so the grievances are never resolved."

"What about a game of chance where both parties agree to be bound by the outcome?" suggests Jeremiah.

"Yes, yes," says Arthur, "a game of chance. A roll of the dice, a card game…."

"A card game, yes. Winner take all," Jeremiah chimes in. "You," here he points to Karl, "you alone must select the game and preside over it."

"And whatever card game you choose, you must act as dealer," Arthur adds.

"Quite right," adds Jeremiah.

"Very well," Karl responds, "you could quite satisfactorily settle this dispute with a card game, and I may even agree to act as dealer. I know many suitable card games. But what about the lady in question? Shouldn't she be told about this contest? Does it not affect her most deeply? Will she agree to be the prize?"

"Does she really…."

"...need to know?" Arthur says, finishing Jeremiah's thought. "Why trouble the poor girl...,"

"...over such trifles?" Jeremiah asks.

"Trifles? Trifles, you say? She must not only be told about this contest, but must agree to be bound by its outcome," Karl declares, his anger rising. "I'm astounded by such callousness! I cannot even consider participating in this game of chance unless I'm assured that the lady agrees to it. Now, which of you is going to discuss it with her and seek her approval?"

Both fall silent, avoiding eye contact with Karl.

When they finally speak, each expresses concern over the wisdom of advising the dear girl of the scheme.

"I simply can't bring myself...." Jeremiah begins.

"...to raise this subject with Tillie," says Arthur.

"Then," Karl announces, "you may count me out."

Both protest vociferously, reminding Arthur of their bonds of friendship with him, their long and loyal service, always reserving only the freshest viands, and the best table in their establishments for him, and their willingness to come to his aid without question. But Karl remains unmoved.

"It's not that I'm opposed to the idea that Tillie should know about the contest," Arthur argues, "it's just that..."

"I can't bring myself to tell her," Jeremiah finishes Arthur's thought. "Would you consider...," says one.

"...taking on this responsibility for us?" says the other.

In the end, unable to resist their pleas for aid, Karl agrees to meet with Matilda and secure her consent to the contest and to be its prize.

Jeremiah and Arthur leave Karl's apartment elated that they not only reached a solution to their dispute over who should possess Matilda, but also that they enlisted Karl's support and participation in the scheme.

Sixteen

What Karl doesn't know, and what I have learned from recent surveillance, is that Wally the Walrus instigated this conflict between Jeremiah and Arthur over Matilda's affections. He befriended both, and over time won their trust and confidence.

In a dingy bar over drinks a few days ago, he engaged in the following colloquy with them, as soon as he saw that each was tipsy. I myself, disguised as a garbage collector, wearing soiled, dull-green coveralls of the type favored by workers of that profession, sat in a dark corner of the barroom recording it all.

"Did you know, Jerry, that our friend Art here has a sweetheart?" Wally asks.

"Really?" asked Jeremiah, a drunken smile on his face. "Why have you never mentioned her to me, Arthur? Are you afraid I'll steal her away?"

Jeremiah was teasing, and Arthur laughed at his little joke.

"Yesh, I've found the mosht beautiful girl in the world," Arthur explains, slurring his words. "And if she agrees to marry me, I shall be the luckiesht man in the world."

"What's her name," asked Wally pointedly.

"Matilda...." Arthur was about to go on when Jeremiah interrupted.

"Matilda?" shouted Jeremiah, suddenly alert and sober. "Impossible! That's the name of my sweetheart, and she's already agreed to marry me."

"My," Wally responded in mock surprise, "what a great coincidence. Are you sure it's not the same woman you're talking about? Ha, ha, ha."

Neither Jeremiah nor Arthur joined in Wally's laughter.

"What's her last name?" Arthur asked, somberly, staring menacingly at Jeremiah.

"Camus," Jeremiah replied.

"Gomez-Camus?"

"The same."

His face reddened with fury, Arthur swung at Jeremiah with a closed fist, knocking him to the barroom floor. Jeremiah leapt to his feet and tackled Arthur, swinging wildly. They thrashed around the floor, upsetting chairs and tables until the brawl was ended by a burly bartender who knocked them both unconscious with a truncheon he kept under the bar. Paramedics were called and both were treated at the scene. Police Sergeant Clouseau declined to arrest either, describing the incident as a case of mutual combat.

Seventeen

As for Karl, the more he thinks about his meeting with Jeremiah and Arthur, and about his promise to meet the woman in question, the more convinced he is that he's on a fool's errand. First, he's never met Matilda, or Tillie as she's called by her ardent admirers. Second, he has no idea whether she loves either man. Third, why would any woman in her right mind agree to be bound by the outcome of a card game?

Nevertheless, Karl makes good on his promise, meeting with Matilda as the clock tower strikes the tenth hour. She's seated on a park bench along the riverfront, smoking a perfumed cigarette and sipping coffee from a nearby coffeeshop.

Both Jeremiah and Arthur, of course, declined even to arrange a meeting for Karl with her. But after providing him with a photo of her, each assured him that Matilda regularly takes her coffee at that very riverside bench, and at that very hour at least one day a week, although, they both agreed, what day of the week she might choose to do so is entirely up to chance.

Luck is on Karl's side. He finds her on his first outing and walks up to her.

"Matilda?"

Karl leans over her expectantly, the warmest smile in his repertoire planted on his face. When she fails to respond, he uses her pet name.

"Tillie?"

She looks up in surprise, apparently unaware of his approach. His first impression of her isn't favorable, since Karl doesn't care for perfumed cigarettes or for the women who favor them, as a rule.

"Hannibal?" she asks, flustered, confusing Karl with the protagonist of one of his early novels.

Perhaps, Karl muses, I should give up Hannibal's long stem pipe and heavy black beard.

She catches her error and blushes.

"I apologize, Mr. Theodore; I have been so taken with that character, his beard, his long pipe, that I've totally forgotten that he's just a fictional character."

Her confusion seems momentarily to have overwhelmed her, and she struggles to regain her composure, extending a hand in greeting.

"Please," Karl replies, taken aback at her use of his nom-de-plume. "I am nothing and I am no one. I am but an empty vessel through whom random fictions migrate. And please, call me Karl."

This nonsensical explanation is enough, thankfully, to set her at ease. They then exchange pleasantries as Karl warms to his task.

"Am I safe in assuming that you love Jeremiah?"

She's at first surprised that Karl knows the man, but after he reassures her that he's a friend, she answers in the affirmative, smiling happily.

Karl is quite taken by her lovely smile.

"And Arthur, do you love him as well?"

"Yes."

Again, her smile tinges the moment with a soft, rosy glow, ignited by the memory of some recent amorous encounter with the ardent Arthur.

Karl has to admit that he cannot discern which yes has the greater probative value on the question of the relative strength of her love for one or the other suitor. But it seems gauche to ask her which lover she loves best. He forgets why the question of which lover she preferred seemed so important.

When I heard him say it, it struck me as utterly irrelevant.

At this point in their encounter, Karl brings up the subject of the card game. How tactless of him not to have prepared her for the shock of what he was about to request of her.

"So, I am to be the prize at a card game?"

Tillie slams her fist down on the bench, spilling her coffee, furious at the explanation Karl offers as to the purpose of his seemingly random encounter with her.

Karl collects himself and remembers four lines from one of Wally's one-act plays, a romantic comedy as it happens.

"Is the result of a randomly selected game of chance any more terrifying than what blind fate may have in store for you? Please, Tillie, think about it. Do you honestly believe either suitor will voluntarily yield to the other? Or do you intend to hold on to the love of both, naively believing that they will accept so hopeless an arrangement indefinitely?"

Four lines, Karl's thinking, four lines exactly; read out verbatim with expert timing and nuance, and with the insertion of her name for that of the original character.

I, seated on a picnic blanket under a tree not far from Tillie's bench, this time disguised as a tae-kwon-do instructor in my bleached white pajamas with black belt, am not as taken with Karl's impromptu performance as is he.

"No," she answers, shaking her head sadly at this suggestion.

"Then, my dear Tillie, it's time to decide. You cannot go on sharing your affections with two such rivals indefinitely."

Karl takes her hand, playing the part of a beloved uncle, hoping to calm her, to reorient her emotions, and begins extemporizing from the plot of one of his novels that was brutally panned by the critics.

"Let me tell you a story about two men not so unlike Arthur and Jeremiah, let's call them Cal and Aron, and let's imagine that they lived somewhere east of Eden. They were siblings, identical twins, actually, Cal was talented, but a failure at everything he tried. Aron was lacking in talent but hugely successful in everything he set his hand to. The world saw Aron as desirable; Cal they saw as troubled and dangerous."

Matilda yawns and begins to fidget with her napkin, looking into the distance at a ferry boat cruising the river loaded with dazed tourists, their tongues hanging out as they blindly aim their digital cameras in her direction.

"Do forgive me," Karl says. "I'm boring you with details, but it's quite a marvelous story. The point I'm trying to make is that these two brothers loved the same woman, yet neither had the courage to submit to some peaceful game of chance to settle the rivalry between them. Instead, they chose to settle their differences by means of a duel, each believing that the use of loaded pistols eliminated the possibility of a chance outcome and favored the more deserving opponent."

Karl now has her full attention.

"The outcome was tragic."

She drops her napkin, her eyes wide with anticipation.

"They agreed to meet at sunrise near the cliffs below Weehawken on the Hudson, a place apparently known for such events. I agreed to act as arbiter, measuring the distance between each of the combatants and assigning to each a stand. I carefully explained that each should fire sequentially, the order of firing to be determined by the toss of a coin. They were both vehemently opposed to any element of chance intervening in their contest, including an innocent coin toss to decide which man should first fire. I had no choice but to accede to their wishes and agreed that I should drop a white handkerchief from my upraised hand as a signal that each was free to fire at will.

"The handkerchief was dropped, shots rang out, and each man fell to the ground in a dead heap, blood spurting as though from a spigot, a bullet lodged in the temples of each."

She gasps, shock and dismay on her face.

"Do you want this outcome on your conscience?"

Her eyes mist over and she swallows a sob.

"No," she whispers, completely subdued and in his power.

"Then you agree to be bound by the outcome of this card game?"

She nods assent, unable to speak, crying softly, her face buried in her hands, her shoulders jumping. He hands her his hanky and leaves before she can retract her agreement.

What Karl does not know, and could not have surmised, is that the woman called Tillie never imagined that Arthur and Jeremiah were two different persons. She had always believed them to be one and the same person, although she could never explain why they would use one name one day and another name the next, attributing the phenomenon to a benign case of schizophrenia.

After she is certain that Karl cannot see her, she smiles and giggles, because, you see, she was secretly delighted that she would never have to confront the problem of choosing between doppelgangers.

Eighteen

Upon a stormy night, at the stroke of midnight, Jeremiah, Arthur and Karl meet in Karl's sitting room where he has set up a card table with three chairs.

Wally, who had learned of the meeting through his network of spies, reluctantly agrees to stay away. He protests, he weeps, he lays hands on Karl, but Karl remains firm and resolute. Wally is not allowed to attend.

Jeremiah arrives first, or at least the one Karl, and I, for that matter, believe to be Jeremiah, and Karl greets him as hospitably as he is able under the stressful circumstances of their arranged meeting.

"Is there any mark on either you or Arthur I can rely on to tell who is who?" Karl asks, taking Jeremiah's raincoat, unsure about which look-alike is before him.

But before Jeremiah can answer, Arthur storms into the entry way through the doorless entrance, wrapped in a halo of rain water which explodes from his raincoat as he pulls it off, spraying the floors, walls and furniture. He advances toward Karl, pushing Jeremiah aside to take Karl's hand.

"My dear Monsieur Karl, my life is in your hands!"

With this, both men enter the living room while Karl tries to tidy up the mess in the entry way. As he carries out this menial task, his mind turns to the game, and to its somewhat complicated rules, taking stock of it most important features.

The game is called vingt because the number twenty figures prominently in determining winners and losers. A forty-card deck is used, all face cards being removed. The dealer deals out one card at a time, the first card goes to the man to the dealer's right; the next card goes to the man to his left, and so on, until a winner is declared.

If the twentieth card dealt is the Three of Diamonds, its recipient wins the game. If, however, the twentieth card dealt is the Three of Clubs, its recipient loses. The odds heavily favor the player who draws the twentieth card since, as everyone knows, the Three of Diamonds is many times more likely to appear on the twentieth draw than the Three of Clubs.

In the event that the twentieth card is neither a Three of Diamonds nor a Three of Clubs, there are other rules for deciding the winner, and Karl considers them briefly, knowing that, in any event, the twentieth card dealt almost always determines the outcome of the game. (Under one such alternative, if, for example, either player holds four consecutive cards whose numbers equal twenty, a 3 plus 5 plus 2 plus 10 of whatever suit, that player will win.)

Obviously, the player to the dealer's left is dealt the twentieth card, which explains why there's usually some initial skirmishing for the chair destined to receive that card. Gentlemen generally resolve the matter with a minimal show of simian aggression. In this instance, as Karl tidies up the entryway, he hears sounds of a struggle coming from the sitting room, heavy breathing, yelps, and groans, chairs scraping, a lamp crashing to the floor.

When he walks into the room, however, it's in near perfect order, the lamp having been restored to its upright position. Although the lampshade is slightly askew, the chairs are in their proper places.

As Karl sits down in the dealer's chair, he looks to his right and sees that Arthur, or the man Karl believes is Arthur, has lost the struggle. Jeremiah has taken the coveted chair to Karl's left; the chair destined to receive the twentieth card.

Karl is not unduly alarmed by the evidence of a struggle between the rivals, since one can hardly be surprised at what any knowledgeable player might do to secure the chair to the dealer's left. Karl has seen much worse in his days as a croupier.

Was I once a croupier? he wonders.

He was indeed a croupier, but it is not my place to remind him of that fact.

Under the rules, all cards are to be dealt face up, it's for the dealer to keep meticulous track of which cards he deals, and players are not permitted to touch the cards, except to ensure that their upturned faces remain visible at all times.

He deals the first card, curious at Arthur's reaction. Arthur, oddly, hasn't even glanced at his card, and seems, instead, to be watching his rival with narrowed eyes.

Karl is struck by the peculiar image before him of two men, identical in every aspect, wearing the same facial expressions, sitting in exactly the same posture, their backs straight, their arms bent at the elbows, their forearms resting on the table, hands clasped together.

"It's uncanny," he mutters to himself.

Jeremiah turns his head to the right, and at the same instant, Arthur turns his head to the left, each looking at Karl at the same angle of tilt, the one miming the other, as if each were positioned before a mirror, their images perfectly asymmetrical.

Karl closes his eyes and practices breathing, just as Dr. Sax instructed *'shoo, shee, shoo, shee, shoo, shee'* until he feels he's in control of his emotions. He resolves to avoid looking at them; he does not want to chance stirring up his fear of mirrors.

"Deal the next card, man!" Jeremiah and Arthur call out in unison.

It occurs to Karl that it was reckless not to have searched each man for weapons before beginning the game. Sweat gathers at his brow, and he struggles to keep his hands from trembling. How will I ever survive this night? he wonders.

He delivers the seventeenth card to Arthur. It's the Three of Clubs.

Jeremiah, to Karl's left, sighs with relief. The one card that could defeat Jeremiah's prospects is gone, were it to have been the twentieth, instead of the seventeenth card dealt.

But the Three of Diamonds is still in play. If that card appears as the twentieth card, an outcome favored by probability, Matilda will be Jeremiah's alone.

Karl deals out the eighteenth and nineteenth cards. Still the Three of Diamonds does not appear. He glances to his right. Arthur's body is rigid, his brow furrowed. Jeremiah, by contrast is smiling, knowing that the probabilities favor him, and that he may soon be declared the victor.

A wave of panic sweeps over Karl, and he resorts once again to Dr. Sax's breathing exercise.

"Dammit man, deal the next card!!!!" both players loudly demand.

Karl works the twentieth card free from the deck, and sends it spinning in Jeremiah's direction.

It is the Three of Diamonds.

"C'est cuit!" Karl exclaims, as he's required to do under the rules.

The game is over! Jeremiah has won the match.

Arthur is glowering at Jeremiah and reaches into his inside breast pocket. Karl braces himself against the edge of the table, ready to run at the first sight of a gun barrel. But, instead, Arthur pulls out a ring of keys and hands it solemnly to a smiling Jeremiah.

"Take these keys," Arthur tells Jeremiah. "They are my house and restaurant keys. I have no further use for them."

Karl is overcome with admiration at Arthur's stoicism.

"Very gracious of you, Arthur," Karl says.

"No, Monsieur, I am not Arthur, but I accept your compliment," Jeremiah says. "He," Jeremiah continues, sneering as he points to the man sitting to Karl's left, "is Arthur."

With that Jeremiah rises and, without another word, heads for the open front door.

"Congratulations, Arthur," Karl says, recovering from his surprise at learning that he'd mistaken one man for the other.

I must confess that I, too, as I observed the proceedings, was convinced that Arthur was Jeremiah and that Jeremiah was Arthur.

"I am the luckiest man on earth!" Arthur exclaims. "But Karl, did you really believe the whole time that I was Jeremiah?" he asks, laughing, not expecting an answer.

With that, Arthur takes his leave, but is no sooner out the door when Karl hears a loud bang, followed by shouting from the street below. Karl rushes to his open front door and scans the street, now filling with curious passers-by. Police and ambulance sirens can be heard wailing in the near distance.

It is clear to any casual observer that as soon as Arthur stepped out into the street, the luckiest man on earth was shot dead by an unknown assailant whom witnesses reported bore a striking resemblance to the victim.

Nineteen

I journey to Oxford to see Tereza. I've long dreaded this journey and have put it off as long as possible. When my train pulls in, I get a taxi, check into a hotel, then head out for Tereza's home.

The grand ante-bellum house with the columns and iron-grill balconies, standing in a grove of magnolias, is just as I remember it. I knock on the door, my heart racing in anticipation. A formally attired butler answers and shows me into the library, then goes to fetch "Miss Tereza." I'm too nervous to sit, and pace to and fro, watching the library doorway nervously, wondering if I've made a mistake in coming here.

The butler reappears and informs that Miss Tereza will be down shortly. He then proceeds into the room, finds a chair in a far corner, and begins to play a medley of Stephen Foster tunes on a banjo, humming softly.

She appears and stops abruptly before entering the library, staring at me.

"Milo?" she says, her eyes wide, as if in shock.

I don't respond, still debating whether to rush past her and out the door.

"Is that really you, Milo?" The Southern drawl in her speech is unmistakable.

"Tereza, please sit," I summon the courage to say. "We must talk."

She approaches me slowly, no doubt wondering why I haven't taken her in my arms. I sit, keeping eye contact, and she follows suit, taking the chair next to mine.

"Is something amiss? Have y'all come with some horrid news, to tell me y'all have found someone new?"

She turns to the butler. "That'll be all, Clarence."

"What a peculiar man. How long has he been your butler?"

"Oh," she says, smiling, "He's no butler. He's my daddy. Thank you, honey," she says.

He turns to us, waves and opens a side door, strumming his banjo and singing *Oh Susannah*! as he exits.

"I have something important to tell you," he clears his throat. "Ahem… I'm not Milo. I'm Milo's double."

"What on earth? Why, that's just crazy …"

He cuts her off, "My name is Franz. Franz Kramer. And Milo now calls himself Karl."

She gasps, gazing at me wide-eyed, her mouth open.

"I don't understand. Why are you saying such a thing? Have y'all gone and lost your mind?"

"I know it sounds absurd. It took me years to accept it. But it's irrefutable. I, and the man you know as Milo, are the same man, each occupying two identical bodies, with a single consciousness."

"Just stop this silly game, hear? We both know what y'all are saying is plumb crazy, going on about doubles and such. Tell me this instant why y'all have cooked up such an outlandish lie!"

"I wish it were nothing more than a game. But it's real. And I will explain as best I can. But before I do, it might be advisable to fortify ourselves with some spirits."

With that, I go to a wet bar tucked away in a corner of the library, get two whiskey tumblers from a glass cabinet, open a small refrigerator under the bar, grab a handful of ice cubes, select a whiskey, and pour. I know where everything is, as though I've lived here all my life. She watches in amazed silence as I prepare our drinks and return to where she and I were seated. She takes the proffered glass, a worried look on her face, perhaps wondering if her poor Milo has become a raving lunatic.

I sit down and begin, "Even though I grew up here in Oxford as did you and Karl, I mean Milo, I didn't know him until I attended that famous prep school in New England. I was a scholarship boy, something of an outcast, and unable to find a friend. I first saw Milo at the commons and couldn't believe my eyes. He was my exact double."

"Ridiculous," she scoffs.

I sigh but ignore her comment and go on.

"What was odd is that no one, except myself, noticed that I was Milo's double. I was not very noticeable and, of course, no one ever bothered with me. I dressed poorly, my clothes and hair were unkempt, and I was housed in the building reserved for the scholarship boys. Milo was always surrounded by an entourage of the most active, rich, and popular boys, and I didn't have money to join in any of their extracurricular activities. He, and the other boys treated me as though I didn't exist."

"A sad, sad story," she says sarcastically. "But it does nothing to prove that y'all and Milo are doubles."

"Very well," I reply, knowing that my story is falling on deaf ears. "You shall have your proof."

I pull an envelope from my coat pocket and hand her a photo.

She gasps.

"Who is that woman standing next to Milo? But it can't be!" she exclaims.

"Yes, Tereza. She is your double, a woman from Prague who looks and sounds just like you. And, if you look closely, you can see me in the background, just behind Milo, wearing a disguise."

I point to the figure wearing a mariachi outfit, a patch over one eye, a bajo sexto slung over a shoulder which, by the way, I play very well.

She holds the photo in a trembling hand, studying each face.

"The fat man is called Wally. He sometimes stays with Milo in Milo's apartment in Alexandria."

Still clutching the photo, Tereza stands and gives me a cold, hard look.

"I don't know what y'all are up to. This photo could have easily been doctored. The only thing I'm sure of is that you're not my Milo. Y'all are some clever imposter who just happens to look like my Milo, trying to deceive me. But I refuse to be drawn into this sham."

"But Tereza, I have important information…."

She cuts me off.

"Get out!" she shouts. "I don't want to hear another word."

"Are you quite sure? I believe Karl, I mean Milo, is in great danger and…."

"GET OUT!!" she shouts, "or I'll have you thrown out!"

Disappointed at having failed in what I believed was a humanitarian gesture to alert the poor girl to Milo's plight, I turn away, hail a cab, and return to my hotel, making a bee-line for the bar where I drink myself into a different sort of starry-eyed, pre-conscious oblivion.

The next day I board a train bound for Alexandria.

Twenty

Karl finds himself in a great city a few hours by train from Alexandria. He knows there is some reason for him to have left the comfort of his doorless apartment, but he can't think what it is. So, there he is, walking briskly through the snowy streets toward the nearest subway station.

I'm worried. I don't know why Karl has traveled to this city. I returned to Alexandria after a disappointing meeting with Tereza just in time to see him leave his apartment for the train depot. I didn't even have time to go home and unpack. It's clear that something must have happened during my two-day absence to lure him away from Alexandria. So I follow closely, quickly donning a Groucho Marx mustache, nose, and heavy glasses in the back seat of a taxi. It was the only disguise I had in my luggage.

The train journey is uneventful, although, as usual, I make sure that no door will impede Karl's progress. On our arrival, I briefly lose sight of him in the crowded train station. Before long I'm tailing him as he makes his way along the bustling, big city sidewalks.

"I don't know why, exactly, I'm searching for a subway station," he says to no one in particular. "I have no intention of enclosing myself hundreds of feet below ground in a sealed subway car, its doors securely closed, hurtling through an interminable tunnel at breakneck speed without any hope of escape. I don't know what I'll do once there, but for now, I'm determined to go where I am meant to go."

A few feet behind him on the noisy, crowded sidewalk, I'm not certain whether what I've heard him as saying aloud was really spoken or merely in his head.

He stops in front of a museum with a grand stone staircase ascending to a bank of massive brass and glass doors. He marvels at the testimony of his eyes. It's a wraith with the face of a woman child. She's barefoot and wears a thin, tattered dress, and nothing but a thread-bare sweater against the cold. A cascade of golden curls spills over her forehead and onto her narrow shoulders.

As Karl mounts the stairs, he sees that her shining blue eyes are the deadened eyes of a blind person, wide open but unseeing. She sings an ancient song in a forgotten tongue, about a fallen shepherd girl who's been deceived by an uncouth ferryman who, for a pittance, bears weary travelers across unmarked rivers and uncharted streams.

Old Occitan, Karl surmises, as he strains to hear the words of her song; it's barely audible above the din of street traffic, the relentless buzz of passing pedestrians, the rumble of trains beneath them, and the whooshing of the wind through the naked arms of giant, frosted trees.

Because she was despoiled by the vulgar boatman, she sings, she's lost her idyllic home, a fallen angel, cast down from heaven. Tears stream down her freeze-reddened cheeks.

There's a basket for donations at her feet, and next to it is a large German Shepard reclining on its paws; her guide dog. Though resting on its belly, the dog is alert and continually scans the passersby who've stopped to listen.

When Karl is within a few feet of the singer, the dog looks up at him with beseeching eyes. He can't resist his mistress's appeal, conveyed through the imploring eyes of this docile beast, and thrusts his hand into his pocket to retrieve a five-dollar bill.

He hands it to the dog who approaches panting, with a glad smile on its steaming, toothy muzzle. He comes up to Karl and sniffs at the five-dollar bill, then growls menacingly.

Karl quickly digs into his pocket to exchange the five for a ten-dollar bill, and hands it to the dog. He sniffs at it, then takes the bank note between his sharp teeth. He carries it to the basket at her feet, gingerly drops it in, and carefully covers the basket to avoid its content's flight upon a sudden gust of wind.

The wraith finishes her song, and bows deeply to her audience, turning her head in every direction, golden curls shimmering in the pale sunlight, and smiles through rosy lips at all who've braved the cold and the snow to hear her song.

Twenty-One

Karl tears himself away, with great reluctance, as the wraith begins another song. He can't help daydreaming about a life with her, that crystalline voice, soothing and caressing, transporting him to fair Elysium, far away. Away from the chaos and confusion, the harsh winter of billowing snow, away from the crowds, away from the doors and mirrors, away from the ominous presence of Wally the Walrus and his machinations, away from the unpredictable Tereza and her many guises.

Karl is torn from these magical images of an alternative life by the push and pull of bodies coming and going all around him. He begins walking, following his instincts, toward what he believes to be the direction of the nearest subway station.

Just then Karl spots him, the man he encountered on the train to Oxford, or was it on the return train to Alexandria? The one who called himself X, the twenty-fourth letter of the alphabet.

He's moving quickly in Karl's direction, as if in a panic, to who knows what destination. His eyes are downcast, and Karl can see that he hasn't yet been recognized.

Maybe I can still avoid him, Karl thinks.

But curiosity gets the better of him, and so he continues to observe The Other as he approaches, ever more certain that it is indeed his one-time train companion.

No one wears his hat at that angle but me Karl muses, and no one mutters curses under his breath as he races down the street in that awkward, half falling manner but me.

Karl has been unable to rid himself of the memory of that encounter on the train to Oxford, and now the random appearance of The Other on the sidewalk of a nameless city, just like that earlier random encounter on the train, is very unsettling indeed.

"Have I reported the train incident to Dr. Sax?" he mutters aloud. He isn't sure because he's uncertain whether his encounter with X occurred before or after his last meeting with Sax.

At that moment, The Other sees Karl, and stops in his tracks just a few feet away, staring.

"You? Is it really you?" Karl calls out to him.

The Other points to himself in response, his gesture answering Karl with an unspoken question.

"Yes, you," Karl repeats, holding his gaze.

He takes a few steps toward The Other, noting the slow backward step The Other uses to restore the distance between them.

Is it possible, Karl thinks, that he has not yet recognized me, that I am to him a random stranger about to commit an assault, an assassin on a hunt for prey?

"The train to Oxford," Karl calls out to him, as if this oblique reference might provoke a memory in The Other.

"I know you from someplace," The Other stammers.

"Don't you remember our encounter on the train to Oxford?"

The Other gapes at Karl, as if wondering whether he should turn and run.

"We're the same person, old chum," Karl says, patting him companionably on the arm.

The Other flinches but doesn't bolt, gazing with an astonished expression of fear mixed with puzzlement.

"How can you say that we are the same person?" The Other asks, bewildered. "I have never been on a train to Oxford, although, if memory serves, I did take a train trip to Alexandria from that place once upon a time. A very unpleasant train trip as I recall it, although why it was so, I'm unable to say. But even so, old man, how does a train ride prove that you and I are the same person?"

"You told me during that train encounter that you're called Xavier. Surely, you'll admit that much."

"Yes, yes," Xavier says, "I do recall an encounter, old boy. But it still doesn't explain why you seem to believe that we are one and the same person."

"Then consider this. You and I look exactly the same, we have the same mannerisms and speech, and we're dressed identically, down to the shoelaces."

Xavier looks down at his shoelaces as Karl continues his argument.

"Come, look into this shop window over here. Here, by my side, old chum. See? Same face, same person, right?"

Xavier stares uncertainly into the window where their images are reflected, side by side.

Karl goes on, calling Xavier's attention to their identical felt hats, the odd angle at which each is set, the blue silk paisley scarf neatly tucked into the identical black overcoats each of them wears, their bushy black beards, the long stem pipes.

"Do you see," he insists, impatient to acquire from Xavier his complete acquiescence in his assertion that he and Karl are the same person.

Xavier listens, continuing to stare into the glass.

"Yes, the images are identical," he agrees at last. "But we cannot possibly exist at the same moment in the same place."

Karl isn't expecting this riposte, which sounds like a veiled threat. If we cannot both exist, Karl thinks to himself, then one of us must cease to exist.

The Other reaches into his breast pocket and Karl draws away from him, ready to flee. Instead of a gun or a dagger, though, he pulls out a small index card and peers at it briefly.

"Do you know where this address is?" he asks, handing Karl the card.

Relieved, Karl takes the card from him and reads it, observing with interest that it's addressed to X, further confirmation, in Karl's mind, of Xavier's identity.

"Yes," Karl replies, "I know it; but it's across the river."

"The river?" Xavier asks. "Which river?" He looks frightened, his eyes wide, as if terrified at the prospect of an impending catastrophe.

"Not to worry, old chum."

Karl does his best to reassure him, hoping, too, that in so doing he might relieve his own growing anxiety. The mention of a river has unsettled him as much as it has Xavier. But Karl puts on a brave face for his benefit.

"Let me hail a cab."

Karl steps out into the street looking for a vacant cab.

Xavier grabs Karl's arm in a panic, pulling him away from the street.

"No! No!" he shouts. "Under no circumstances are we to take a cab! We must take the subway! It is imperative that we do so!"

"Why?" Karl is baffled at Xavier's insistence on taking a noisy, foul-smelling and claustrophobic underground train when a comfortable cab ride would easily suffice.

"Because we must!" is Xavier's emphatic response, his eyes dark and, if there is such a thing, dead in their sockets.

Then Karl remembers that he was himself hurrying to the nearest subway station before running into Xavier without a clue as to why he was doing so, or where he expected the train to take him, or why, given his documented januaphobia gravis, he should ever wish to be in so confined a space.

That riddle is now solved by the smudged and frayed index card with its penciled address. Karl returns the card to Xavier who tucks it back into his breast pocket.

"Very well, follow me," Karl says. "I was just on my way to the nearest station when I ran into you, old chum."

It occurs to Karl that he's never been on a subway train in this or in any other city, and that he hasn't the foggiest notion where the nearest station is. But some instinct pulls him onward, with his helpless doppelganger in tow.

Xavier locks his arm in Karl's as they make their way down the busy sidewalk. At last, arm in arm, they reach the cavernous hole in the sidewalk with concrete steps leading down to the unseen train platforms below. Karl grasps the railing, suddenly incapable of forward movement, fighting vertigo. Xavier tugs at him in an effort to lead him down the stairs into the gloom.

Karl finds relief by looking away from that open pit leading down to who knows what fate. He spies a tavern across the street, its door invitingly open to the public.

Xavier continues to tug at Karl's arm, trying to drag him down into the darkened station. Karl ignores him, tearing away violently, and hurries across the street. He suppresses a scream as he careens toward the open doors of the tavern across the street. Running, he glances over his shoulder just in time to see the top of Xavier's head descending into the gloomy, forbidding subway station.

I, still in the guise of Groucho Marx, must decide whom to follow, either Xavier down into the subway or Karl into the tavern. Then, just as in the church courtyard at Karl's ill-fated wedding, my mind separates from my body, which slumps to the ground. The Groucho Marx glasses, nose and mustache slide noiselessly to the pavement.

Outside of its body, my conscious mind divides, ghost-like, half of it follows Karl, the other half falls in behind Xavier. I suddenly understand why the brain is divided into hemispheres.

Karl sighs with relief as he makes his way through the opening into the tavern, while Xavier disappears into the bowels of the subway station.

"I should feel remorse at abandoning my companion, but all I feel is joyous liberation," Karl says aloud.

Twenty-Two

Just inside the tavern, Karl's eyes adjust to the darkness as his panic subsides. He scans his surroundings. Seated alone at a far table is a nearly naked, but for a ragged loincloth, stoop shouldered, hoary, old man, with pointed ears and flaming eyes. On the table before him rests a bottle of cheap whiskey next to a half-empty glass. Behind him, leaning against the wall is a battered, discolored wooden oar.

To his left, Karl spies an ancient, cadaverous woman with wispy white hair, clothed in frayed mourning attire, sitting at an upright, out of tune piano, playing Pavane pour une enfant défunte far too slowly and with much too little bass.

"She has no left hand," Karl mutters.

Badly in need of a drink, he takes a seat at a table as far from the hoary, with age, boatman as possible.

"May I?" says another person, who's dressed like a banker. Without waiting for a response, he pulls out a chair and sits at Karl's table.

Karl recognizes his riverfront café companion, Zeke, and nods in acknowledgement. He doesn't bother to speak since he and Zeke's minds have connected and are exchanging greetings. The following dialog occurs entirely in their heads, as each reads the other's thoughts.

"I believe I've just narrowly escaped death," Karl is thinking.

"No one escapes death," Zeke thinks back.

Karl, still in need of a drink, signals to the barman, a large fellow resembling Wally the Walrus, droopy mustaches and all. But for the apron covering his prodigiously, protuberant paunch, he could be a dead ringer for Wally.

The barman saunters over to the table, and Karl orders a bottle of whiskey and two glasses. The barman nods and returns to the bar to fill Karl's request. But instead of whiskey, the barman returns with two bottles of Tigris and Euphrates beer, made in Nineveh. When Karl points out the barman's error, he retrieves the bottles, uttering unintelligible curses, goes back to the bar and loads a large, donut shaped clay vessel through which his arm passes, onto his shoulder. Thus laden, he returns to Karl's table, sets two large clay cups down and pours what smells like whiskey from the donut shaped clay vessel.

Karl thinks that further complaint is futile. Zeke agrees. They drink their Hittite spirits in silence which is broken by the sound of the skeletal crone who begins to play Claire de Lune on her rickety piano. It's then that Karl notices the severed left hand of the pianist resting on the top of the upright piano.

The bartender, who is beginning to look more and more like Wally the Walrus, joins them with his donut shaped vessel laden with Hittite spirits. He sits heavily and raises the mouth of his earthen vessel for repeated draughts of his Hittite brew. No one speaks, although the barman begins to chuckle to himself. Karl and Zeke notice that the boatman, too, is chuckling, and winks at them.

"I'm beginning to feel very uneasy," Zeke is thinking.

"Me too," thinks Karl in reply.

"Like something bad,"

"...is about to happen," Karl thinks, completing Zeke's thought.

The barman suddenly draws a truncheon from his apron and, with lightning speed, knocks both Zeke and Karl semi-conscious.

Out-of-body, I am powerless to come to their aid, and watch in horror as the boatman and the bartender drag Zeke's and Karl's senseless bodies into a dark room behind the bar and drop them into an open pit.

As for me, I feel my consciousness begin to dissolve, and hear the sounds of rushing trains and the desperate wailing of human suffering.

Twenty-Three

Xavier watches Karl run toward an open tavern across the street.

"I am well rid of him," he tells himself. "I have a rendezvous to make at an address across the river."

With only half of my conscious mind, I follow Zeke as he starts down the stairs. When he gets to the bottom of the stairs, he takes stock of his surroundings.

The cavernous place he enters is dimly lit by fluorescent lights that flutter on and off, many of them permanently off. Through the gloom he finally makes out a ticket booth and, just beyond it, a bank of turnstiles. He's not yet at the train platforms. The air is damp and heavy, and everywhere the incessant, deafening rumble and screeching of trains coming and going permeates and wounds the atmosphere.

Hesitantly, Xavier approaches the ticket booth. He taps gently on the window to attract the attention of the sleeping ticket master. She looks up, obviously annoyed by his intrusion into her nap time, pulling a curled fist from her moistened undergarments.

"Yes?" she demands with scorn written upon her shriveled, scowling face.

"Please, may I ask? Which train must I take to get to this address?" He pushes the address card through the slot in the ticket window.

She looks at it impatiently.

"Where did you get this card?"

He doesn't know how to answer her because he doesn't know how he came by it.

"Can't say?" she asks, sneering. "Never mind, just hand over the fare."

She points to an amount on the fee schedule nailed above the ticket window.

He passes the currency through to her, and she hands him two heavy tokens, one of silver, the other of brass.

"May I have my address card?" he asks, pointing to the card he unwisely surrendered to her.

In response, she tosses the card over her shoulder.

"What address card?"

He walks away to avoid any further unpleasantness. Fortunately, he committed the address to memory. He passes through the turnstiles which open when he deposits a token into the coin slot. Somehow, he knows that the brass, and not the silver token is to be used to gain entrance.

Once through the turnstiles, he sees three tunnels before him. He peers into each, hoping that he might see something in one or the other tunnel to help him decide which to enter.

The one to his left leads to a landing where yet a deeper, angled stairway descends.

The tunnel to his right is like the one to his left, it leads to a platform deeper into the bowels of the place.

The middle tunnel is blocked by a turnstile labelled Stairway to Heaven, which leads to an upper level platform. He likes that name and inserts a silver token into the coin slot. His token is rejected. He notices a grimy brass plate indicating that a gold token is required for admission.

He ponders whether to return to the surly ticket master to get a gold token. But even with that token, he worries, what certainty do I have that the Stairway to Heaven will lead to my destination?

Out-of-body, I'm powerless to render aid, but certain that Xavier is on a path to destruction. It's painful to watch, knowing that I should have uncovered this scheme long ago and averted this catastrophe.

In a state of confusion, Xavier is startled by the feel of a comforting hand on his elbow, and by the deep reassuring voice of its owner.

"Can I help you, Pilgrim?"

Xavier turns to face a very large, outrageously large man with overgrown mustaches that droop down past his chin.

"Thank goodness. I was at wit's end!" Xavier exclaims. "I don't know which tunnel to take."

"Where are you bound?"

Xavier recites the address from memory.

"All I know is I am to cross a river to get there."

"You mean, Pilgrim that you hope to cross under the river. We're talking about subway trains here, Pilgrim, not river barges. And that address happens to be a berth at the Port across the river where folks board their vessels for an Atlantic crossing."

"A sea voyage?" Xavier asks, amazed at such an unexpected destination.

"Only one stop, Pilgrim. Well, let's get going!"

He turns into the tunnel and Xavier follows. They begin a descent deeper into the depths of the station as the light dims to the glow from a single candle held at arm's length. The once white tiles of the passage downward are dark with soot and filth, covered with graffiti and an endless array of crudely drawn, lurid sexual images.

As they descend, the noise increases, not just the sound of screaming trains but the added sound of human voices wailing and moaning in the distance. Xavier wants to turn and run, but the nonchalance of his guide is reassuring.

At last they reach the bottom of the stairway. Xavier squints into the darkness before him.

"You've made good progress, Pilgrim."

Xavier feels like a condemned man on his way to the guillotine with a sack over his head, waiting for the moment when a heavy blade should fall, severing mind from body.

As they round a sharp bend, a single, blinding floodlight illuminates a foul smelling, littered platform where a line of decrepit train cars from the dawn of the last century rest. Xavier brings the scene into focus with difficulty.

First, he sees a small, wraith-like woman-child with a halo of golden hair singing a song of destruction, promising a fiercer, more tormenting hell on earth. Her seeing eye dog snarls and snaps at the cowering masses clustered around her.

Next, he sees a stooped but tall, gaunt man with pointed ears and fiery eyes, wearing only in a loincloth, shouldering an oar, barking out orders to a cowering group of men and women, some crying, some laughing, some howling, some tearing at their clothes, their eyes, their hair. Here and there random couples engage in a variety of unconventional sex practices with shocking abandon.

Xavier averts his eyes in horror and disgust, and cups his hands over his ears in a futile attempt to block the deafening din around him.

The man with the long oar continues to shout in some Germanic language Xavier doesn't recognize, although the meaning of the words is clear. He's commanding the condemned to board the waiting train cars, swinging his oar at those who try to slip away from the passenger queue.

Meanwhile, the wraith continues to sing in a shrill voice which rises above the clamor of the huddled masses, telling of a place where sin is encouraged and crimes are rewarded, beckoning the masses forward into the waiting cars, their doors wide open.

Xavier's guide, who momentarily strayed from his side, approaches.

"Give me that silver token, Pilgrim," he commands.

Xavier obeys, and his guide leads him to the nearest car and pushes him in, after handing the silver token to a spritely gargoyle. Xavier stumbles into the car and begins to look for a seat. But this is a club car, reserved for the Hollow Men. Xavier knows, immediately, he's not permitted to sit there.

He moves on to the next car, passing The Hunger Artist on his way. The Hunger Artist is performing an auto da fe and is just then raising a silver chalice.

"Drink from this, all of you, it is the cup of my blood," he intones, although there is but a single congregant kneeling before him. He takes no notice as Xavier gingerly glides past him into the next car.

There, on the nearest bench, two identically looking men are seated; identical except where the eye socket of one should have been there is a large, gaping hole, as if honed out by the invasion of a large caliber bullet.

When he sees Xavier, the one with the hole in his eye socket holds up a playing card for Xavier's inspection.

It's the Three of Diamonds.

Then the other gentleman, the one without the hole in his eye socket, rises to greet Xavier, announcing that his name is Jeremiah.

Why this stranger has given Xavier his name, or spoken at all, strikes Xavier as strange and unnatural. Yet he seems intent on being Xavier's companion. After introducing him to the mute with the empty eye socket, he leads Xavier to a young lady who sits smoking a perfumed cigarette. She rises abruptly upon seeing Xavier, and bursts into song.

"Quando me'n vo' soletta per la via, la gente sosta e mira" she sings. She struggles to keep her balance as the train car lurches forward, holding onto an overhead handrail. "E la belleza mia tutta ricerca in me, da capo a pie," she continues, oblivious to the chaos all around her. ["When I walk alone along the street, people stare and admire my beauty from head to toe."]

Whereupon Jeremiah, about to tumble from the sudden movement of the train car, cries out, "Legatemi alla seggiola!" ["Tie me to the seat!"]

Xavier moves away from Jeremiah and his entourage. In the next car he spies Zeke and Karl. They greet him smiling.

"Ubi is est qui olim eram?" asks Zeke. ["Where is he who I once was?"]

"Plus tard, les delices de la damnation seront plus profondes," Karl recites, to no one in particular, as Xavier approaches him. ["So long as one lives, one must put off the pleasures of Hell."] Xavier ignores Karl and moves on to the next car.

There he next sees a short, bald, pudgy man, naked except for the pince-nez on his nose. When the short, bald, pudgy man catches sight of Xavier he rises from his seat and approaches.

"You must be seated, comrade, we're getting under way," Dr. Sax says.

He takes Xavier by the hand and leads him to the front of the train car. He stops before a body, slumped lifelessly on a bench.

Following Xavier through the train cars, ghostlike, I gasp, seeing my own body, yet, unable to take possession of it with my conscious mind. Weeping, I realize too late that I, too, am a victim of Wally's nefarious scheme.

Xavier, who hears my weeping, is transfixed, gazing at my mindless body, unable to move. Dr. Sax pulls him away and leads him to the last bench at the front of the car. To Xavier's surprise, he sees that Tereza and her double are already sitting there holding hands, although neither takes notice of him, and when he addresses them, they pretend not to hear him.

Twenty-Four

The train picks up speed, and Xavier clutches at a handrail to avoid falling. It speedily moves into a pitch-black tunnel. He can neither see nor hear anything around him.

Oddly, the rocking motion of the train car gives way to a rolling, pitching motion. Slowly it dawns on Xavier, as it dawns on me, that we are no longer on a train. We are aboard a ship of some kind.

We are on the top deck of an ocean liner, gazing out upon a vast sea of possibilities and identities under a starlit sky, sailing into the darkness, into that starry oblivion of preconscious night, all together in plurality, yet apart in flash-point singularity.

Author Profile

This is Conrad Aragon's debut Novella. As a lawyer (University of Chicago JD) and retired judge (Los Angeles Superior Court), and a student of literature (MA, Yale Graduate School), he has been writing for a very long time. He lives in Los Angeles, California U.S.A.